Praise for *USA Toda*
Crane's psycholo

"You are not prepared for the twists...Pamela Crane has in store for you. The schemes...are sure to have you at the edge of your seat." – *POPSUGAR*

"Crane succeeds at painting families and friendships in vivid detail; women will see their tussles and triumphs in these pages, and will relish the twists and moments of brave camaraderie and bold revenge... A satisfying read that has echoes of Liane Moriarty and of Emily Giffin's *All We Ever Wanted*." – *Booklist*

"Pamela Crane's anthem to female friendship and the empowerment of women proves one thing. Friends will do anything for each other...including lie, cheat in bed, and kill. This novel is a read for our tumultuous times." – Jenny Milchman, Mary Higgins Clark award-winning author of *Cover of Snow* and *The Second Mother*

"One of the most chilling opening scenes I've ever read, and the tension keeps right on building. My advice: don't read this book...unless you're prepared not to put it down until you're finished!" – *New York Times* bestselling author Wendy Corsi Staub

"I loved it! It's so well written, with sharply observed characters and the kind of fast-paced, twisty plot that keeps you turning the pages..." –*Sunday Times* and international bestselling author Debbie Howells

"There is always great depth to Pamela's writing and this is no exception." – Bestselling author Patricia Dixon

"A captivating mystery with prose that fans will devour." – Literary Lover Reviews

IF
ONLY
SHE
KNEW

IF ONLY SHE KNEW

PAMELA CRANE

Tabella House
Raleigh, North Carolina

Thank you for supporting authors and literacy by purchasing this book. Want to add more gripping reads to your library? As the author of more than a dozen award-winning and bestselling books, you can find all of Pamela Crane's works on her website at www.pamelacrane.com.

For Jess and Em,
my teenage ride-or-dies that I would face any curse for.
Long live our nineties memories.

The Diary of Cordelia Bloodson

June 27, 1836

It is a sensation more potent than knowledge, a suspicion stronger than truth. I can feel it claiming me—death, that is.

The contractions grow intense today. The baby is pushing his way out, searching for bright freedom from my dark, swollen womb. Yet something feels wrong. The pain is as heavy as my heart, but it is not the discomfort of childbirth. It is altogether something different.

I have seen a change in my husband, an anger untapped until recently, and I fear I will not be on earth much longer to pick up the pieces of Reginald's inevitable destruction.

The ghost of my father visited me in a dream last night. Or perhaps it was a nightmare. The two have been intertwined as of late. Father brought a warning that something terrible is about to happen that will bring ruin to my home and disgrace to my family. How can I bring a fifth

1

child into a world so full of evil?

I spoke of my concerns to Reginald, but he is convinced that I am simply worrying in excess. Our family physician, Doctor Edgar Valance, suggested I might be afflicted with hysteria, but for the sake of my family, I must not lend credence to that diagnosis. With Reginald's increasingly mercurial behavior and my own grieved heart, I must wonder if despair is contagious. I have felt it coming for weeks now, that unexplainable fear. And yet I am a helpless victim to it.

So I open the bedroom window, invite in the salty June breeze, and distract myself with the view. The raging blue ocean as it devours the jagged shore. The dense forests full of vibrant green life. The rocky slope of the cliff climbing up to meet the field of fragrant flowers. And my colorful little garden where I have buried my secrets.

I shall not write of those, lest it sour my mood.

Instead I gaze at the maddening ocean and feel it drawing me to its briny depths. I recall what my father, who lingers on my mind, once told me. That my name, Cordelia, means "heart, or daughter of the sea," named after King Lear's sympathetic daughter. Did not Father realize she was hanged at the end of the play? I pray my name does not presage the fate the sea has planned for me.

I must go, as my contractions wage war on my flesh. Yet

a final thought haunts me, corrupting the beauteous sight and luscious smells of the garden outside my window. These are all mere places to inter my body. An earth that is primed to eat my bones and feast on my flesh.

I know only one thing: my end is near, perhaps today, and no one believes me.

Prologue

June 27, 1997

When you're the descendant of one of history's most notorious killers, you're born with a dark mark. No matter how far you try to run from the reputation, it always catches up to you in the looks you get when people connect the dots between you and that infamous name.

Jack the Ripper. Lizzie Borden. Ted Bundy. And then there is Reginald Bloodson, the man who left my family legacy in ruins.

As if being related to a killer wasn't enough, add to that a curse passed down for generations, and you spend your whole life with a scarlet letter plastered on your chest. The town of Bloodson Bay blamed my ancestor for the unexplained mysteries that happened every year, on this very date, June 27, for as long as anyone could remember. But that's not the worst of it.

When a murder happens in your own backyard and you're forced to cover it up…well, there's no coming back from that. That kind of thing condemns the soul.

No matter how many secrets I buried, or how many lies

4

I shoveled to cover up the truth, the truth is always underneath.

Waiting. Biding its time. Reaching to drag me down with it.

The summer of 1997 I fell into that pit so deep I wasn't sure I'd ever claw my way out.

It should have been my summer of freedom. Self-discovery. Love. At least that's what it was for every other girl. But not for me. Mine would be the summer of terror. Grief. Death.

Sometimes I wondered if bloodshed was my birthright. I was the too-many-greats-to-count-granddaughter of Reginald Bloodson: founding father of my hometown Bloodson Bay, and the man whose killing spree spawned ghostly legends since 1837.

On June 27 of that year, exactly 160 years ago, he snapped and murdered his family. And he's been haunting our town ever since.

Tonight's the anniversary. The perfect night for a ghost story. Except that it isn't just a story. It's my history. A history that's catching up to me, hungry for blood.

Chapter 1

The campfire sparked and crackled within its ring of moss-covered rocks along the forest's edge. Damp air clung to the canopy of leaves above us, dangling tiny pearls that caught the moonlight. A light fog draped the field, curling wispy tendrils around tree trunks.

Two downed trees hugged the firepit, serving as seats for me, my younger brother Chris, his best friend Jonah Reynolds, and Jonah's little sister Tara. We all stared transfixed by the golden flames, listening to the bullfrogs bellow and crickets chirp.

A nearly empty bag of marshmallows rested on Jonah's lap, and a box of graham crackers was tipped over beside a Hershey's chocolate bar wrapper where a single rectangle melted to the silver paper. I had delivered on my promise of s'mores if they stuck it out until midnight. But tonight I was giving them so much more.

The boys had requested a story—a ghost story—but not some silly old fable about Bloody Mary emerging from a mirror, or a one-armed lumberjack serial killer. No, this was *my* story. A true story. The story of how my family had committed murder long ago, and continued to murder even today.

Holding a flashlight under my chin, my voice cut through the cool June air, a low whisper on the breeze:

"Bloodson Bay is a haunted town. A cursed town. A plague to all who live here. As with all curses, there was a beginning. And we're all still waiting for the grisly end."

Tara and Jonah exchanged a fearful glance, while Chris rolled his eyes with boredom.

"Ooh, *grisly end.* Way to dramatize it, Peace," Chris said, waving his hands in mock fear. His concert T-shirt that he'd bought at a Bush and No Doubt concert last year hung loose on his prepubescent frame, all skinny arms and bony legs and knobby knees. My dad's never-ending farm chore list had yet to beef up my brother's muscles.

"Chill out, Chris," Jonah came to my defense. "You're being a buzzkill."

I nodded in quick gratitude and began the story of the family curse I had never *really* believed in—not until this summer, anyway—a curse that was coming to fruition this very moment. Only I didn't know it at the time.

"The year was 1837," I continued, "on a night much like tonight." The words held my campfire prisoners captive. "The wind whipped the tree limbs. The ocean pummeled the beach. And a man named Reginald Bloodson stood alone at the very same cliff beyond those woods."

I pointed toward the dense forest that spread for over two hundred acres, eventually opening up to a clearing overlooking the bay. The infamous Bloodson Bay, one of the southeastern coast's only overlooks surrounded by miles of flat sandy beach.

"While Reginald admired the violent ocean, his thoughts kept returning to the house he had built, Bloodson Manor, where his wife Cordelia had bled out in their bedroom, in the very bed in which he slept."

Myth or not, I had never ventured to the spot I spoke of, where the sea met the rocky cliff at the edge of our family property. It was also where Bloodson Manor still stood.

"As Reginald gazed at the raging waves below, he mourned his dead wife. Then he reflected on all that the past twenty years had brought him since first arriving in North Carolina. His mind wandered back to the day he first set foot on this wild, untamed land. He vividly recalled how he had farmed the sprawling fields, harvesting cotton that would turn this town into a thriving farming village. He reminisced fondly about the first day his eyes rested on the beautiful face of Cordelia, and how he instantly fell in love with her."

"Eww, c'mon," a voice interrupted. I turned to Chris, watching a grimace contort his baby face where a dusting of facial hair had begun sprouting only within the past couple weeks. I had seen his new razor in our bathroom and teased him mercilessly about it.

"Are you ever capable of shutting up?" I grumbled.

"I thought you were telling us a ghost story, not a *love* story."

Beside him Jonah shifted nervously, not nearly as disgusted by the idea of romance, it seemed, as his gaze fixed longingly on me. I had suspected feelings emerging the more he hung around my house, pretending he was there for my brother.

"Whatever, major loser," Jonah retorted, throwing his fingers up in the shape of an M, then W, then L. "We all know you're a romantic at heart, the way you're jonesing for my sister."

My attention slid over to Tara, realizing that it wasn't heat from the flames that flushed her cheeks.

"Can we let Peace finish telling her story, please?" Tara pleaded.

I observed my listeners, so naïve to the evils of the world. I was on the cusp of adulthood, but my parents (to my eternal chagrin) still treated me like a child. As much as I hated to admit it, I was still a babe in the woods—despite the self-assured facade I presented to the world. I wouldn't enjoy that blissful ignorance for long.

"As I was saying, Reginald had loved Cordelia more than anything. Everything he did was for her. But his love demanded a great cost—their very lives."

A mosquito pricked my leg and I swatted at it. The edge of my Dr. Martens rubbed the skin raw on my bare ankle. A storm earlier that afternoon had cooled the summer air, bringing a chill that caused me to wrap my flannel a little tighter around my baby doll dress.

"He loved her so much he killed his family?" Jonah raised a skeptical eyebrow. "I'm not buying it."

"Jonah, every great tragedy is born out of love." Tara pressed her palm to her heart. "Try reading Shakespeare instead of watching *The Simpsons* and you'll learn something."

"Anyway," I spoke loudly over them, "Reginald thought back to when Cordelia first took possession of his heart, when he had built a house for her on the cliff overlooking the bay. He had taken her to see it, proposing on one knee. Her kisses were all he needed to know that she loved him as much as he loved her."

Chris contorted his face, puckering his lips and making wet kissy noises while Jonah cracked up beside him.

"Knock it off," Tara chided them with an unchallenged authority. "I think it's beautiful."

"I bet you wish Chris would kiss you like that," Jonah teased his sister with a cackle.

"Shut up! I do not!" Tara folded her arms across her chest and huffed.

Chris elbowed Jonah in the rib. "I bet you wish Peace would kiss you like that."

"Both of you, grow up!" I interceded. "I'm just getting to the good part." I aimed the flashlight at each of their faces, blinding them one by one with the beam.

"Shortly after their wedding, Reginald and Cordelia

created a home together, enjoying sunrises from their ocean view and watching their land flourish. Then they started a family, adding one, two, three, four children—all boys, God help them—to their happy little fold. While pregnant with the fifth, Cordelia sensed something was wrong. So she warned Reginald that if anything were to happen to her, he should raise the boys to be compassionate and loving like he was. He promised; of course he agreed to her every request as he kissed her cheek."

This was when the story got bleak, and I lowered my voice to a tense whisper.

"But in the real world, happily ever after does not exist. As Reginald stood on that precipice under the moonlight, his memories turned dark as the sky as he remembered the day Cordelia betrayed him. It was the night she died, one year earlier."

The flames grew higher, thicker, more vibrant as I spoke. Three pairs of eyes watched me. But out in the inky black beyond our circle of light, hidden by the shadows, I felt another presence, watching with an unnerving intensity.

"It happened during the birth of his fifth boy, on that fateful June 27, when Cordelia did not survive childbirth. While the baby lived, Reginald found he could no longer keep his promise to Cordelia. Soon his crops wilted. His home deteriorated. And his heart broke more each day. He shrunk into a miserable man, full of anguish and despair."

11

An owl screeched in the distance, joined by a chorus of coyotes. The kids exchanged soft whimpers, but I pressed on.

"On the one-year anniversary of Cordelia's death, Reginald could no longer look at his children, for they wore his beloved's eyes, her nose, her lips, her smile. So he gathered his sons and led them to the cliff's edge. One by one, he pushed them into the watery abyss below. Then he leaped onto the jagged rocks, and at last his broken body joined his broken spirit."

Across from me jets of flame danced in Tara's glistening eyes.

"That day, the blood of the children stained the bay red, so the townspeople named the town Bloodson Bay. It was an apt name. The name of a man, and a token of his awful deed."

I leaned forward, resting my gaze on each kid—Jonah, then Tara, then my brother—and raised a single finger. "But one child survived the fall. He grew up to continue his father's legacy, eventually building a family of his own. A family cursed with death. You see, every year on the anniversary of his father's death, the townspeople felt the haunting. The pull of the cliff. And for decades after, pain plagued that very day: June 27."

I paused for effect. "This. Very. Night."

Everyone grew quiet. Even the orchestra of bugs fell under the hushed spell.

"Legend has it that every year on this day someone in

12

Bloodson Bay dies a horrible death," Chris warned.

"For real?" Tara looked to me for confirmation.

Straddling the fallen tree log, the bark still damp from the rain, I nodded, flashlight aimed up at my face. "It's true."

"Enough of the ghost stories, or Tara will end up sleeping in our parent's bedroom," Jonah ragged, reaching down at his feet. "Let's chill."

On the ground beside his Reebok Shaqnosis tennis shoes—sporting a hideously mesmerizing design of concentric rings—was a Sony boombox. He pressed a button, pumping Notorious B.I.G.'s "Somebody's Gotta Die" into the air.

"Hey, who changed my CD? I had Foo Fighters in there," Chris complained.

I had warned my brother against joining the Columbia House record club, advertising eight CDs for a penny, but Chris never listened to me.

"How do you know so much about this curse?" Jonah asked.

"Because it's our family, duh," Chris replied.

Jonah's eyes widened. "What do you mean? You're related to Reginald Bloodson?"

"Damn skippy. You know our Uncle Bernie—Bernie *Bloodson*. How *didn't* you know Bloodson is our last name? Well, it *was* our last name until we changed it to Christie."

The name change was purely for our safety, our dad

13

always insisted. Alas, my poor brother—*Chris Christie*—never got a vote on the matter, though he was the only one paying the price for it from the constant teasing, which to his mind was worse than any Bloodson curse. Cracks like: *Your parents must have been pretty lazy or stupid to use it twice.* I mean, it *was* pretty redundant.

I once asked Dad about it, and his reply: "If it worked for Kris Kristofferson, then it can work for your brother." I didn't know who that person was, but apparently he was famous.

As for my name…well, my parents weren't hippies by any stretch, but since I was born at the tail end of the 1970s, I had a sneaking suspicion they just might have come up with that flower child moniker after smoking a doobie, and hoped I would live up to it. The joke was on them. From the beginning, their headstrong (and sometimes hardheaded) daughter had given them very little *peace*.

"How would I know your last name was Bloodson?" Jonah retorted. "It's not like you ever said, 'Hey, just so you know, the last name you've always known me by, *Christie*, isn't in fact my real last name. It's actually *Bloodson*.'"

"So that means you've got a psychopath in your family history." Tara aimed the comment at Chris while struggling to open a Butterfinger wrapper.

"Yep, I guess so." Chris took the candy from Tara, easily ripped it open, chomped on the end, and handed it back to her.

"Hey!" she exclaimed.

"I call bull on the whole Bloodson relation." Jonah shook his head in disbelief. "You're messin' with us."

"We're not lying," I insisted. "This property you're sitting on was the original parcel that Reginald built his house on."

"So why did your family change your name?"

"Because we didn't want to get cursed!" Chris blurted out.

"No, that's not why," I corrected. "With my dad running for mayor, he didn't want a last name that was tied to bloodshed. Although Reginald's own son kept the last name, the family eventually abandoned the house because they didn't want to be tied to the curse. They were pretty superstitious back then."

"They still are," Chris whispered.

A somber hush floated across the darkness, and I wondered what fears lurked in their imaginative minds.

"I've been there, you know," Chris spoke after a moment. "Bloodson Manor."

"You've seen the *Slaughter Shed*?" Tara gasped.

Over the years the local kids, raised on slasher flicks, had taken to renaming Bloodson Manor the *Slaughter Shed*—a way cooler name, I had to admit.

"I've more than seen it—I went inside!"

"When?" I asked, shocked that my brother had hidden that from me.

"Last year. Exactly one year ago tonight."

15

"And?" Jonah wondered aloud.

"And what I saw was too horrible to talk about."

"Prove it," Jonah dared.

"How am I supposed to prove it?"

"Take us to the house."

The challenge hung between the two boys, tense and sharp. An uneasiness wrapped around us, but no one wanted to break its hold.

"I can't," Chris finally answered.

"I knew you were lying." Jonah abruptly stood up, nearly catching the hem of his wide-leg skater jeans on fire.

"No, it's not that I *can't*. But if you saw what I saw there...you'd never go back either. I'm telling you, the curse is real. I saw it with my own two eyes."

"What exactly did you see, Chris?" Tara probed.

"You wouldn't believe me if I told you."

Tara reached over and cupped his hand. "Try me."

Chris sucked in a breath, overcome by the only person who could crack his shell. "If I tell you, promise me you won't tell anyone else."

Now I was beginning to get worried. What secret could my brother possibly be keeping from me? "Is whatever you saw really that bad?"

Chris's voice wobbled with a terror I'd never heard from him, a guy who rode wild steeds in rodeos, and who'd once, armed only with a baseball bat, chased off a pack of coyotes menacing one of our colts. "I'll never forget it no matter how hard I try. It still haunts my nightmares."

And then my brother told us something so unbelievable, so chilling, that it felt like the devil's breath was stirring the hairs on my neck.

Chapter 2

As the legend of the Slaughter Shed passed along from child to child, the details of the house where Cordelia died grew more sinister with each retelling. More decrepit with each version. More murderous with each imagination. It was a twisted game of Telephone as images of a ramshackle clapboard building stained red with blood slipped from the tongues of storytellers, but no one had actually ever laid eyes on the house.

Except my brother Chris, apparently.

"It was already nighttime when I got there," Chris began, a tremor in his voice, "and I almost didn't go inside, but I couldn't back out at that point."

By now the campfire began dying out, its blue and orange blazes smoldering down into an angry red heap of embers. Above us thunderheads strained at the seams of the sky.

"Why couldn't you back out?" Tara's voice was barely above a squeak.

Chris puffed out a scoff. "I had been dared."

I thought that by middle school the double-dog-dare would be considered passé. Apparently for some boys—

and some immature men—it represented the currency of manhood right up to high school and beyond.

"Who dared you?" I wasn't going to let whoever was behind this off the hook.

Chris waited a beat before answering, kicking a pebble with his Birkenstock sandal.

"It was the Valance brothers."

Now *that* complicated things. I could almost hear myself gulp.

"Those turds Victor and Leonard?" Jonah spat as if their mere names tasted sour. "I didn't think you were friends with them."

"I wouldn't say we're *friends*. They were making fun of me for being, uh"—he grinned self-deprecatingly—"vertically challenged, so when I stood up to them, they dared me to take them to the Slaughter Shed. When they told me to go inside, I couldn't say no or else I'd get bullied for the rest of my life."

My brother often got picked on for being in the shallow end, so to speak, of the gene pool. Over the years I came to his defense, usually involving a knuckle sandwich or two. Some people lived up to their name, but I, *Peace* Christie, did not.

"So what did you see when you went in?" Tara leaned toward Chris, attention fixed eagerly on his every word.

Though I didn't want to admit it out loud, I was just as excited to hear what he saw. As a tomboy who'd always been considered *one of the guys*, I could be pretty tough.

19

But tough enough to venture into a place dubbed the *Slaughter Shed*? Even I had my limits.

Chris glanced warily at the woods behind him as if something were waiting for him. He returned his gaze to us, the remnants of the fire casting a buttery glow on his boyish features, then he continued.

"When I opened the front door, it was really quiet. At first it seemed like a normal vacant house. Creaky floors. Furniture covered with sheets. Dust everywhere. But then I saw…" Chris stopped. Shook his head. "I can't."

"Chris, what did you see?"

Coming from the boy who watched *I Know What You Did Last Summer* without flinching, and could play a *Resident Evil* video game marathon on autopilot, he had a pretty high horror tolerance. Whatever he had witnessed had to be pretty bad.

"I saw…a body, Peace. Dangling from the rafters."

My jaw literally dropped. "What? Are you sure?"

"No, that's just it. I'm not sure what I saw. It was just…swinging there. I didn't see a face since it was so dark and its back was facing me. But my brain couldn't make sense of it. It seemed unreal. And the more I stared at it, the more I thought maybe it was a ghost or something."

"That's bunk!" Jonah interrupted. "You believe in ghosts?"

"I didn't before, but I do now! How else would you explain it?"

"Did you try touching it to see if it was…like, fleshy?" Jonah poked his finger in the air in demonstration.

"Heck no! I ran like hell. I don't know who it was, or why it was there, but I wasn't about to touch a dead body!"

If indeed my brother had seen an actual corpse, we needed to find out who it was…and why it was there. This wasn't something he could just run away from and pretend never happened.

"Why didn't you tell me? Or Mom and Dad?" I asked.

"Would you have believed me if I told you I saw a ghost hanging from the ceiling?"

I shrugged. "Probably not a ghost, but a person, yes!"

"I'm still not buying this story." Jonah leaned back, shaking his head.

"I'm telling the truth!" Chris shouted, edging up to Jonah like he was ready to fight for his honor.

"You know there's only one way to find out if you're full of shit," Jonah tossed back at him.

"Don't even say it." Tara stood up, dusting off her no-nonsense Gap khakis that matched her no-nonsense personality. "Nope. No way. Never. If you dare go there, I'm gonna bounce."

Then Jonah rose to his feet, staring his sister down. "Are you going to tattle on me to Mom and Dad if I *do* go, Tara?"

"I'm trying to protect you, Jonah." Tara rested a hand on his shoulder, attempting to reason with her unreasonable brother. "Someone might have been killed

21

there. You have no idea what you're walking into."

"Exactly." Jonah shrugged her hand off. "Which is why I need to find out. If you're not coming with, I'll go to the Slaughter Shed by myself. But one way or another, I need to know if there really was a body or not. I have my doubts."

Chris, the resident horror maven, rose in his own defense. "Even if the animals got to it," he pointed out, eyes gleaming, "there'd still be a skeleton hanging there. With tattered rags and scraps of flesh clinging to it. Yum-yum." He made a creepy slurping sound like Hannibal Lecter eating somebody's liver.

"You are one sick bastard," said Jonah. "And if you're trying to scare me, it ain't working. I'm going. Anybody with me?"

"Are you crazy?" Tara grabbed his arm, pleading. "You want to venture out into the woods, at night in the dark, on the anniversary of the Bloodson massacre when *everyone* knows there's a curse set out to kill someone…and you figure it might as well be you?"

This whole debate was getting out of hand.

"Yeah, I agree with Tara," I butted in, remembering it was me who was the oldest and therefore in charge, not some hormone-hopped-up teenager with a death wish. "It's not safe."

"Look, Peace, there's no curse, just like there's no body," Jonah insisted. "And I'll prove it. C'mon, the moon's bright, I've got an extra flashlight. It'll be…an adventure. Imagine you're Zelda on a quest or something."

I didn't want an adventure. Not the deadly kind, at least. But Jonah was *the* most stubborn guy on earth, so it was either fight him or join him. And we all knew which one was easier in the long run...

"Fine," I conceded, "I can't let you go alone. But if I say leave, you better freakin' listen to me!"

"Deal!" Jonah applauded.

Out of an abundance of caution I doused the dying campfire with what was left of my Wild Cherry Pepsi. Grabbing my flashlight, I aimed it toward the wood line where a gaping hollow in the bushes led to a path through the thicket...and into the biggest regret of my life.

Chapter 3

Thorns snagged my dress. Branches scratched my thighs. And don't get me started on the hole torn through my Lilith Fair concert tee.

I hadn't dressed for a wilderness exploration, and it was evident that Chris, leading the way, hadn't either, as mud caked the socks he wore with his sandals.

While Tara and Chris debated which was the best power couple from *Beverly Hills, 90120*—of course it was Dylan and Brenda, not Kelly and Brandon—I had a bad feeling we were walking in circles.

"Didn't we pass this tree already?" I asked.

I could have sworn the tree looked familiar, with its split trunks. A small hole where they joined almost looked like a face creepily watching us.

"I don't think so," Chris replied unconvincingly.

I had no idea how far back the property ran until it met the bluff. And to be honest, I hadn't cared until now. All I knew was that I was trusting Chris, who could barely navigate his way home from Blockbuster, to lead us through the pitch-black wood with only the moonlight and Jonah's flashlight to guide him.

"Are you sure you remember how to get there?" Tara sounded more worried than me.

Whisking my flashlight back and forth across the path, the thicket seemed to grow denser with each step. The woods felt ominous, alive. As if it were conspiring against us.

"I don't remember it being that hard to find before. I just followed the horse trail until it met a huge tree where the path split off. Then instead of following the footpath, I cut a left and the clearing wasn't much further beyond that."

A huge tree. That sounded specific. *Not.*

"So where exactly is this tree you speak of?" Jonah piped in.

"It should be close. We're still on the horse trail, aren't we?"

"It doesn't look like a trail to me." Poor Tara sounded like she was about to pee her khakis.

A scrape on my leg began to throb. The snap of footsteps trampling brush somewhere in the dark riveted my feet to the spot. Anything could be hiding within the forest's depths.

I leaned down to retie my shoe when a whisper floated to my ear.

"Danger..."

My spine zipped upright. Put a fork in me, I was done.

"Did anyone hear that?" I dared ask.

"Hear what?" Jonah called over his shoulder, where

Tara and Chris flanked him up ahead.

Flashing my light this way and that, the pale beam passed over shadows and movement rustling the leaves underfoot, but I couldn't locate where the voice had come from. I felt more than saw something shifting, shaping itself from the shadows.

A coyote's howl echoed, joined in by its pack, sounding closer and closer. A breathy huff broke through the din directly behind me, and I screamed and stumbled backwards as I pivoted around. The flashlight whacked against a dark form racing toward me, and the next thing I saw was a blink of light before I plunged into darkness as the flashlight slipped from my hand, dropping to the dirt before clicking off.

My mind shut down. My throat closed. My legs numbed. It was as if I could feel the curse coming for me, and I was its helpless prey.

Then my brain jumpstarted my survival instinct as I shrieked and ran.

Chapter 4

The night was a blindfold. And everyone knows you don't run wearing a blindfold…unless you want to get hurt. As my chest smacked into something hard that had blended in with the darkness, and I fell back butt-first onto the packed earth, I learned that lesson the hard way.

I was too shocked to give thought to whatever had scared me in the first place as I lay on my back gazing up through the branches at slivers of starry sky above.

"Peace, are you okay?" Tara came to my rescue while Chris and Jonah simply stopped walking to laugh.

"Yeah," I said, grabbing Tara's hand to pull me up. Wet leaves and mud stuck to my calves. "Not sure *they're* going to be okay after I get done with them." I tossed a glare at the boys, whose laughter only grew louder.

"That looked brutal, sis." Chris barely pushed the words out as he leaned over, clutching his stomach.

I lifted my hand, palm facing him. "Talk to the hand."

Shaking the last of the leaves from my clothes, a word slit through the air behind me.

"*Danger…*" it warned.

This time it was more than a whisper.

27

"Guys, listen! Did you hear that?" It couldn't just be me hearing things...could it?

Chris and Jonah fell silent as we all strained to listen.

"I think I heard it too," Tara breathed. "*Danger?*"

So I wasn't losing my mind after all.

"Who's there?" Jonah yelled into the trees. Nothing answered back. "If you don't show yourself, your ass is grass and I'm the lawnmower!"

I rolled my eyes. As if anyone would take the threat of a 115-pound wannabe thug seriously.

The crack of a branch jolted us all to attention as we pivoted toward the sound. "Danger!" a voice boomed.

This time we all heard it and scuttled together.

"Okay, I believe you," Chris whimpered.

It took a moment for my brain to recalibrate, but something felt familiar. I knew that voice. And then it all clicked.

"Uncle Bernie?" I called out. "Uncle Bernie, I know it's you!"

A second later the warm sound of his hearty laugh greeted us as he stepped out of the brush, slapping his hand on his thigh. "Gotcha! I can't believe ya'll fell for that!" He wiggled his fingers at us, pursing his lips in an *O* shape as he attempted to replicate a ghostly "oooooohhhh, dangerrrr" between chuckling.

"You asshat!" Chris scolded. "I almost peed myself."

"That's not something you should admit out loud, son," Uncle Bernie replied.

28

My dad's brother reminded me of a younger, beer-drinking Santa. Pink-faced and jovial, gut mushrooming over the waist of his Wrangler jeans, too much untamed facial hair. The stark similarities even earned him the nickname *Uncle Santa* among the kids, along with the annual unpaid job of serving as town Santa every Christmas season. It was hard not to like a person who listened to wet-bottomed, runny-nose children's endless Christmas gift lists with a merry *ho-ho-ho*. He was the type of guy who could defuse a fight with a joke, and would come to the aid of any Tom, Dick, and Harry who needed a hand with something.

"You scared the shit out of us, Uncle Santa," Jonah confessed.

"Hey, language, kid." Uncle Bernie wagged a reproving finger at Jonah, but his sloppy grin said he was probably too drunk to mean it. His shirt crookedly hugged his torso, as if the buttons were off by one.

Jonah ignored the chastisement, considering every other word out of Uncle Bernie's mouth was usually a cussword or a variation of one, depending on how plastered he was.

"What are you doing out here?" I asked.

"I could ask you the same."

"We're trying to find the Slaughter Shed," Chris explained.

"The Slaughter Shed?" Uncle Bernie's face twisted with confusion.

29

"The old Bloodson Manor." Then I added, "The house Reginald built."

Uncle Bernie's grin drooped to a frown. "I had a feeling that's why you kids were wandering around out here. Why you fixin' to venture to that ramshackle place?"

"We're just curious about it, that's all."

"It's a bad idea, I'm telling you." The usual mischievous sparkle left his eyes. "Don't you know what tonight is? It's the anniversary of the family's death—the day of the curse. And everyone knows that Reginald's ghost haunts that house, especially tonight."

No number of years or scientific logic could wash away the stain Reginald Bloodson had left on our town. Every old-timer and newcomer believed in the curse, then spread it through gossip.

Whether the curse took a life every year on this date, or someone took it upon himself to execute the curse, it all had the same result: perpetuating the mystery. It was the plight of living in a small town where superstitions never died, and crazies walked undetected among us.

"I don't know about all you, but I'm still going." Jonah had barely finished the sentence before picking up his stride and following the path away from us.

"I'm not letting you go alone," Chris declared, chasing him.

Tara and I exchanged a glance, shrugged, and trailed behind them.

"Don't say I didn't warn ya!" Uncle Bernie called out

30

behind us.

The closer to the overlook that we got, the more the wind wound its way through the trees, pulling last winter's leafy remnants down to their earthy graves. Above us the canopy became so dense it blocked any stray moonbeams from reaching us. Every little crunch and crack sent a startling ripple effect through me.

By the time my legs were sufficiently aching, Chris cheered our arrival. Too sticky sweaty in my flannel, I took it off and wrapped the sleeves around the waist of my dress, instantly embracing the cool air.

I stepped into a clearing, and the wide, endless sky confronted me with a breathtaking view. The vast expanse of the ocean made me feel so small and insignificant, its heartbeat thrumming against the bluff's face. Its depths warned of all the lives it had stolen throughout the centuries, and the lives it would continue to suck the last breath from.

"Whoa…" Jonah gasped, eyes fixed on something behind me. "There it is."

I turned around. Tucked into a patch of grassy land bordered by an overgrown garden was a huge, impressive Colonial—not a shed at all, like the rumors depicted it. Certainly nothing I would call the *Slaughter Shed*.

The tales about the Slaughter Shed weren't even close to true. I had always imagined a rundown bare-bones dwelling, something more like one of the old-timey clapboard houses we'd seen in those historic towns where they performed Civil War reenactments. Certainly nothing like this three-story dwelling with a double-decker porch and dual stone fireplaces flanking each end.

Vines clawed their way up its wooden siding, as if the building had grown out of the earth with them. A lonely makeshift swing composed of a hand-hewn log and thick rope swung from a nearby sycamore, its bark peeling and trunk hunched, as if it had spent its life taking on the burden of a strong gust. At its base the roots were exposed and intertwined, like a nest of snakes.

"C'mon. Let's go inside," Jonah urged.

Nothing felt right about this, but I couldn't let superstition stop me. We had made it this far, after all. If anything, we could prove there was nothing to fear and put Reginald's ghost to rest. Finally end the Bloodson Bay curse.

With Jonah in the lead, we wandered through an overgrown flower garden, their sweet scent perfuming the air. I picked a single bloom, fascinated by its beauty, and tucked it into the front pocket of my flannel.

Up close, the house revealed nature's toll on it. Blotches of moss clung to the porch. The columns listed to one side. It was as if the cockeyed house remained standing through sheer force of will. The steps groaned as we mounted them one at a time, as if our weight caused them physical pain.

The second to last step gave way under Tara's foot with a loud crack, and her leg disappeared through the board. Her scream pierced the air. I swung my flashlight toward her, finding half of her swallowed by the stairs. Chris grabbed her arm, pulling her out of the rotted hole in the wood.

"Are you okay?" he asked, leaning down to examine her.

After catching her breath, Tara brushed off her pants. "Yeah, I'm fine. That just scared me, is all."

We all treaded much more carefully after that, every footstep testing the boards. When we reached the top step, Chris froze, unable to move forward. "I can't go in there."

"Yeah, I don't feel good about this either," Tara agreed, latching onto his arm.

"It's just a house, sis," Jonah said. But I heard the fear in his voice. Even he had his doubts.

"No, I'm telling you, it's haunted."

"I promise there's no body hanging from the rafters," Jonah tried to assure Chris as he shoved his way past me toward the massive front door.

Resting his hand on Chris's shoulder, Jonah stopped long enough to whisper for him to man up and stop being a sissy in front of Tara. "No girl wants a guy who can't take care of her," he warned.

"Yeah, little bro," I added. "Girls like a guy who's in control. We want to feel like you'll take care of everything. When you lose that respect, you lose the girl."

Our advice seemed to work, because a moment later Chris's back straightened up as he feigned a whole new level of confidence that his wide eyes betrayed.

"*Tell me what you want, what you really really want,*" Tara sang softly.

"I really really want to get out of here," I muttered.

Chris turned to Tara and laughed. "Are you singing Spice Girls?"

She grinned and sheepishly cocked her head to one side. "It's better than the creepy silence."

"Whatever floats your boat," Chris said, cupping her hand in his. Girl Power seemed to do the trick for both of them, considering the shy grins on their faces as they clung to each other.

I joined Jonah at the front door as he turned the handle, pushing hard against the swollen wood that wouldn't budge.

"We need to all push together," I suggested.

All four of us took a step back and on the count of three we thrust forward, slamming our shoulders against the door together, delivering all our weight at once. The door heaved open, scattering us into a pitch-black entryway. I fumbled about in the fitful moonlight for something to prop open the door with, lest a draft should suck it shut. A brass umbrella stand containing a moth-eaten umbrella and a moldy cane did the trick.

"Good," I said with self-satisfaction, "now we won't get stuck in here."

A breeze followed us through the entryway, stirring up the dust. Quicksilver-gray clouds formed huge mushrooms across the sky, blocking the moonlight from filtering through the windowpanes, some nearly opaque with decades of grime.

My first instinct was to skim the wall with my flashlight beam in search of a light switch, but then it dawned on me that the house's construction predated electricity and it had never been updated with modern conveniences. And even if the joint ever had electricity, it would have long since been turned off—duh!

Standing sentry ahead of us were two banisters framing a floating staircase with several steps missing risers and others missing the tread. I led the group past the staircase toward the living room, where exposed beams crossed the ceiling.

"I remember this room," Chris said as he took Jonah's flashlight and scanned the space. "This was where I found the body—or ghost or whatever."

Jonah's fiery bravado must have shrunk as he sidled up to me. "Look, no body. You probably imagined it."

We explored the first floor, shining our flashlights over sheet-covered furniture, just like Chris had described, and examined the intricate details of the house—the two large marble-encased fireplaces, the elegant molding—more mausoleum now, in its crumbling glory, than mansion. I ran my fingertips across the floral-patterned wallpaper, the fabric a thick linen-cotton blend, nothing like the thin, papery neon-geometrical-patterned wallpaper in my bedroom. As I headed deeper into the dining room, my light caught the edge of a discolored piece of floorboard. Moving the beam across the plank, I realized what I was looking at.

A large circle of rust-red blood.

"Is that...?" Jonah leaned down to examine it. "Holy crap. It *is* blood!"

I knelt to get a closer look, reaching out a finger to touch it. Slightly wet. When I lifted my finger, a tiny red circle dotted the skin.

"Oh my gosh, it's fresh! This happened recently!"

"Do you think someone was murdered in here?" Jonah stood up, pacing back.

It didn't seem like nearly enough blood to be a crime scene. "I don't think so. It's just in one spot. If someone was murdered here, don't you think there'd be a lot more blood in a lot more places?"

"True..." But Jonah didn't sound convinced.

Though what did I know about blood spatter? Or ghosts hanging from rafters? Or anything that might have happened in this old, creepy house? Everything about this felt like an *X-Files* episode, which after tonight's sci-fi-adjacent experience, I wasn't sure I would be able to watch anymore. Regardless of what happened—or didn't happen—the more I stayed, the more I wanted to go. Everything about this place, especially in the dark, was urging and pulsing for us to leave.

But then Tara's voice cut through my dread with an even darker urgency:

"Guys, you're not going to believe this, but Chris wasn't imagining what he saw…"

Chapter 5

Tara was right. I couldn't believe what I was looking at. Above her head, wrapped around the rafter, was a rope, similar to the one used for the tree swing outside. Exactly where Chris said he had seen the body hanging.

I reached up to grab it, its frayed tip dangling just out of reach. Jonah jumped up and grabbed the end, but the rope was too securely wrapped to break free. Dropping back to the floor, he shrugged. "Nothing's gonna break that loose."

"This looks like proof that whatever Chris saw wasn't a ghost," Tara's stare fixated on the rope, "but something very very real."

"Okay, so then where's the body?" Jonah asked.

"Maybe someone took it down." As I said this, a barrage of thoughts followed. If that was the case, it meant someone else had been here since last year...and clearly covered it up. And if someone covered it up, that begged the question if it had a been a suicide...or something more sinister. Like murder.

"Who else could have been here? This house is on our private property, and way out in the woods," Chris added.

"Plus the road here from town is way overgrown, probably too much for a car to make it through."

At one point long ago, a dirt road had connected the main street in town to the coastal homes, with Bloodson Manor the very last home along the path. Over the years, when electric was brought in, the road was paved, but because the house had been left vacant, it wasn't included in the pavement project. Eventually the dirt path fell into disuse, recognizable only to "meddling kids" like us, primed for a mystery worthy of *Scooby-Doo* and the gang. All we needed was a Mystery Machine and we'd be Bloodson Bay's answer to Daphne, Velma, Shaggy, and Fred. (I, of course, most identified with Velma, the brainiac.)

"None of this makes sense. If someone was murdered, wouldn't we have heard about a missing person report last year? And how do you have a hanging body last year, but wet blood that is recent?" The problem was Tara was trying to apply logic to an illogical scenario. "Bodies don't just disappear out of thin air."

Except in Bloodson Bay, apparently.

"And the plot thickens…" Jonah whispered conspiratorially.

"Why don't we just drop it?" Chris cut in. "There's no reason for us to worry about it since it doesn't involve us."

"Someone is dead, Chris," I objected. "There's a rope that a body had been hanging from, a corpse that's missing, and bloodstains on the dining room floor. We can't ignore the facts. Somewhere out there is a family wondering where their loved one disappeared to. The least we can do is tell the police."

"Tell them what?" Jonah asked. "That our friend thought he saw a dead body a year ago but it's gone now? You think the cops will take us seriously?"

"It's worth a try."

Chris rushed up to me, facing me toe-to-toe. "No way. I'll tell them you're lying and that I never saw anything."

"What's the big deal with telling them?"

"You don't think they might assume I had something to do with it by not mentioning it for over a year? I obstructed justice, or whatever it's called, by not saying anything! I could go to jail!"

Tears swelled in my brother's eyes, and I realized he was terrified. While every other teen his age worried about which teacher they'd get for algebra next year—even atheists turned to God if He could keep them out of Mr. Scarey's math class (and yes, that was his legit name and reputation)—my brother was worried about going to jail.

"Chris is right," Tara interjected. "We learned about this in my government class. They recently passed a law that made not reporting a dead body a crime. A year in jail and $1,000 fine."

So that threw a monkey wrench into things.

Jonah gawked at his sister. "Wow, teacher's pet much?"

"But he's a juvenile," I reasoned.

"We can't be sure that will get him off the hook. Especially nowadays. You've heard about the Central Park jogger case with all those kids getting convicted...and there wasn't even any evidence against them!"

The early nineties had birthed a new legal precedent of kids being tried as adults. There was no way to know what they'd do to my brother. Plus with our dad being the mayor, they might even want to make an example of Chris.

"I'm not willing to take that risk." Chris folded his arms. End of story.

But no matter what they said, if it had been my family member missing, I'd want to know. Solving this was the right thing to do. The family waiting for answers, the person who died, they all deserved closure.

If I was going to get to the bottom of this, I needed to find out who went missing last year, which would require several days stuck in the library's microfiche room. Then figure out why someone would have removed the body, then hope that led me to where the body was now. And that didn't even cover whose blood stained the floor...

This was way bigger than me.

"You guys do what you want, but I'm not letting this go." Chris's mouth dropped open, ready to argue with me. "But I promise not to go to the police...yet. If I figure out who died and what happened to him—or her—I'll make sure to leave your name out of it."

"What's all this *I* stuff?" Jonah asked. "Obviously I'm going to help you. You'll need my brawn."

41

Jonah thrust his hand out, palm down. I placed mine on top on his.

Then Tara added her hand, smirking at Jonah. "And you'll need my *teacher petness.*"

With a grumble Chris pressed his hand on Tara's. "And you'll need my…Tom Cruise-like athleticism?"

We all chuckled at that, standing there a moment, our pact sealed through our joined hands.

"Tom Cruise is way taller than you, pal," Jonah sniped good-naturedly.

We all chuckled at that, standing there a moment, our pact sealed through our joined hands.

"Maybe there are some clues or evidence here that can help us." Tara looked around, lighting up corners of the room with her flashlight. "Let's split up and see if we can find anything."

"Good idea," I agreed.

"I'll go with Peace." Even in the dark I noticed a sly smile cross Jonah's lips.

"And I'll go with Tara," Chris said a little too eagerly.

I aimed the flashlight at Tara and Chris. "Alright, you two search the first floor. Jonah and I will head upstairs and explore."

Jonah recklessly sprinted up the staircase ahead of me, heedless of danger, disappearing into the darkness. Climbing the stairs, I examined the portraits lining the walls on both sides of the stairway. They appeared to be family portraits, presumably of various Bloodson

42

ancestors who had lived here. Reginald, Cordelia, several children's portraits, among others.

From what I remembered, Reginald had raised his four sons in this house until Cordelia died during childbirth. A year later he murdered his children, with the fifth baby the only survivor. According to legend, the infant had been taken in by Reginald's sister, who raised the child in this same house until he came of age to take a wife and make the home his own.

The details of the manor got hazy after that. Apparently on June 27, 1867—thirty years after Reginald's death—their oldest son's body was found at the bottom of the crag, in much the same way as his father. Some speculated he slipped and fell; others say Reginald's ghost pushed him over the edge. The cause of death was never determined, but the legend of the Bloodson curse was born that day.

"Peace! Come here!" Jonah shattered my contemplation, his voice muted and distant.

I carefully searched the second-story hallway, checking each bedroom. All eerily quiet.

The first couple bedrooms that I passed were filled with furniture and toys that fit various children's ages. Rocking horses. Wooden blocks. An antique Noah's Ark playset with pewter figurines. But the next bedroom drew me inside, as it clearly belonged to a husband and wife.

Narrower and shorter than beds parents shared nowadays, the ornate four-poster frame was a glossy mahogany brown. A disturbing thought followed me around the room. Cordelia had possibly died in that bed. In the corner a white nightdress hung from a headless metal mannequin, the yellowed fabric rustling ghostlike as I swept by.

It was a little too creepy for my taste.

"Where are you, Jonah?" I called out to him as I left the room.

But he didn't answer. I kept walking ahead, the sound of my heartbeat thrumming in my ears. As I reached the end of the hallway, the one side of the wall was replaced with a railing as it opened up to an overhead view of the dining room. Directly below me was the pool of blood.

At the end of the hall, I nearly walked face-first into a closed door. Reaching out, my hand touched the doorknob. It turned in my palm, but I wasn't the one doing the turning.

"What the he—" I muttered.

Suddenly the door swung open, pushing me backwards. As I stumbled into the banister, I lost my footing and felt myself falling.

In a moment of freefall my arms began circling as I tried to find my balance while my body leaned too far over. Just as I expected to plummet, an unseen force broke my fall. A hand fisted my shirt, pulling me back to my feet.

By the time I found Jonah's face in the darkness, I couldn't stop myself from jumping into his arms.

"You saved me!"

He held me tightly until I peeled myself out of his

grasp. "After almost killing you. Let's call it even."

Guiding me away from the railing, he pointed me toward the door that he had emerged from.

"I wanted to show you something." Jonah stood at the bottom of a stairwell that led up to the attic. "Do you hear that?"

I listened but only heard the still-frantic breaths coming from my lungs.

"I don't hear anything."

"Just wait and listen," Jonah urged, stepping on the first step, then the second.

For a long moment the air was dead silent, and then I heard it. A dull scratch. Then another one, like something was clawing at the ceiling above us.

"It's probably rats," I guessed. "I'm sure the house is crawling with critters."

"No, that's not what I heard. Give it a minute."

He took another few steps up.

"What are you doing?"

"Going to investigate," he stated matter-of-factly.

"Are you crazy? Didn't you ever read *Flowers in the Attic?* No way am I letting you go up there alone."

"Suit yourself. It's your funeral."

"I sure hope not," I murmured.

Together we climbed the stairs. It was dark as ink, the depths hidden from the pale moonlight barely seeping in through a lone window at the top. Only the flickering beam of my flashlight lit the corners, and I wondered how much life my D batteries had left.

Jonah led the way up the narrow stairwell, barely wide enough to proceed single file. At the top the ceiling left little room for me to stand, forcing me to hunch over slightly while Jonah's greasy Kurt Cobain hair brushed against the underside of the roof. A bedroom sat on one side of the large space, with what appeared to be a makeshift bathroom at the end of the attic.

"This must have been where the housemaids lived," I speculated.

The room was a pack rat's dream, packed with all manner of furniture, bric-a-brac, and miscellaneous crap. Maybe even priceless heirlooms, but it was too cluttered to know for sure. I passed my flashlight over a rolltop desk. And a loom. Then a thin, pale face looking directly at me. His smile was contorted, evil, and I saw bloodlust in his eyes.

I screeched at the sight.

"Calm down! It's just a painting. See?"

Only now did the gilded edges of the frame come into view. I might have been jumpy…just a little.

Jonah approached the painted figure, head cocked with curiosity, drawing my attention to the backdrop of distinctive white flowers…framing such a hideous face.

"I wonder who that is…"

Jonah passed his fingers along the edges of the frame.

"Hey, shine the flashlight right here," he instructed, pointing at the bottom corner. Painted in crisp black letters was the name *Gertrude Bloodson.*

"Who is Gertrude Bloodson?" he asked.

"Beats me. Maybe we can find out."

I wandered further into the room, finding more furniture, some covered in cloths and others covered in dust. On a small table I found an ornate wooden box. Judging by the style, it looked like an early nineteenth-century Swiss musical jewelry box. My grandmother had one very similar.

Lifting the lid, soft music poured out as a ballerina twirled in circles. While she pirouetted to her melody, the first thing I saw was a huge gold locket, almost the size of my hand. I picked it up by its chain, brushing my thumb over the jewel encased in the oval front. I pried the locket open, but instead of finding a photo, a folded piece of paper was tucked inside.

"Peace, help me open this!"

I was fairly salivating to read the note, but Jonah sounded almost frantic. I returned the locket to the jewelry box and found him standing at the foot of a large chest with a sheet draped over one side. He was tugging on the lid with all his might. I joined him in the task, and seeing it was futile, pointed to the huge lock on the front.

"We need a key."

As I aimed the flashlight around us, willing the key to magically reveal itself, a loud thump boomed from the belly of the house.

"That is no rat," Jonah concluded for the both of us.

"We need to go." I was done with all of the noises and near-death falling and blood spatter.

Grabbing Jonah's hand, I dragged him toward the stairs leading back down to the second floor. He pulled back, resisting.

"No way. We're just beginning to find cool stuff. Imagine what else is up here. You wanted to solve that murder. Well, here's your evidence room!"

I had almost been won over, when another thump, louder than the first, changed my mind. We bolted for the stairs, taking them two at a time. Near the bottom of the steps I slammed into the wall as I cut the corner too close, snagging the sleeve of my shirt on a knob sticking out.

"Wait, I'm stuck!" I yelled to Jonah, who was already halfway down the hall.

Yanking on my shirtsleeve, I ripped it free, jarring a flapping wooden door open with it. A linen chute—similar to the one we had in our house, but much wider. I almost didn't give it a second thought as I began to close the small door then stopped short. Something looked strange about it.

There was a noticeable gap next to the chute. With something inside.

A secret compartment! I reached into the slender opening, my fingers dragging through sticky cobwebs, past crunchy dead bugs. At least I thought they were dead until I felt the scurry of tiny legs.

When my fingers finally wrapped around the object,

and I realized what it was, a gasp escaped my lips.

Chapter 6

During my senior year of high school, while rewarding myself for winning first place for a story I'd submitted to the Young Writers of America Competition by enjoying an evening of *Dragon Warrior*, I had come to realize a sad truth:

I had no direction in life. I hadn't applied to any colleges. I had no drive for a career path. My future looked dismal at best.

I was in the middle of defeating Dragonlord with a HurtMore spell when my mom found me in our basement rec room.

"Do you think I'm a loser, Mom?" I had asked her.

"A loser? Heavens no. You're one of the brightest kids I've ever known."

Brightest kids. That was Mom's euphemism for nerds. Truth to tell, I had *always* been a nerd. For most of my childhood this served me well. Nice to everyone. The one my classmates wanted to copy homework off of. And I lived for Honor Roll and Debate Team.

"Oh, Mom, you're just prejudiced." I sighed with exaggerated world-weariness. "When I'm an old maid of forty-five I'll be living in this crummy basement, working at Wet Seal selling clothes to overprivileged teen girls."

"Knock off that kind of talk, Peace. You should be proud of yourself. You just won a major writing competition!" She gestured to the cheap plastic trophy sitting on the concrete floor at my feet. "You've got talent to burn!"

Yeah, so I'd been told. All through school I'd gotten high marks on every essay and composition and short story I'd ever turned in. Some of my teachers gushed that I'd be the next Agatha Christie. That was flattering, but when I looked back at the pimply scribblings I'd filled umpteen journals with, it was all I could do not to laugh—or throw up. The notion of my having a career as a serious writer seemed preposterous.

"I appreciate what you're saying, Mom, but writing well is *hard*. And very few people make a real living at it. On top of that, I'm just not…driven."

"Not driven? First of all, you've gone through—what? nineteen levels?—to defeat Dragonlord in that video game. If that's not driven, I don't know what is. Secondly, what makes you think you've got no future? We all have a different version of the future, and not one is necessarily better than the other. All that matters is that you find something you enjoy doing and do it."

Then she said to me, and I would never forget it, "When you can't find opportunities, opportunities will find you. You just have to keep your eyes open."

51

At this very moment, in this creepy house, holding the one thing that might be a clue to what happened here, my eyes were wide open. An opportunity had fallen into my lap...or hands, as it were.

A spider had hitched a ride on the cover of the leather-bound book I pulled from the hidey-hole. I held the volume up to my lips and blew, sending the creepy-crawly flying amid a galaxy of dust that danced briefly in the flashlight's beam before disappearing in the blackness.

With a frisson of excitement, I gently peeled the book open to the flyleaf, where I read the inscription *Diary of Cordelia Bloodson.* Page upon page of neat cursive entries filled the book, with dates scrawled across the tops of most pages.

I imagined Cordelia writing by lamplight, her fountain pen in hand, dipping the nib into the inkwell as she organized her thoughts and committed them to the page. It was hard to believe that I held the musings of a woman from 160 years ago.

"I thought I heard you scream that you were stuck." Tara seemed to materialize out of nowhere.

"Good thing I wasn't actually hurt or else I'd have bled out by the time you got here."

But Tara was too busy looking over my shoulder to respond. "What did you find?"

"It's Reginald's wife's diary. This is amazing. It's been perfectly preserved, too."

As I scrolled through the pages, Tara hovering over

one shoulder and Chris approaching behind her, I recognized names and pieces of information that could complete the puzzle of Cordelia's life…and death.

"She talks about Reginald, and her pregnancy. Even her doctor. This could explain a lot of what happened back then. The whole origin of the curse."

"That's cool and all, but that won't help us find the body that was hanging downstairs," Chris reminded me. "You know, The Case of the Missing Dead Guy that you want to solve?"

Maybe Chris was right. In my excitement for uncovering a piece of history, I had forgotten what we were supposed to be looking for. Clues to a death that happened last year, not last century.

I continued skimming across words and bits of phrases, but the more I read of the diary, the more I was left with a strong sense of foreboding.

"Listen to what Cordelia wrote on June 1, 1836, a month before her death," I said, reading an excerpt aloud:

"I have seen things I cannot explain. A haunting set out to kill me. It lives here, in our very home, and I have no way to escape it. I fear it is coming for me, and soon."

"Maybe this is connected to what Chris saw. She predicted her death, guys. She even said whatever it was *lived* in this house."

"So you're saying you think this house is…" Chris

ventured.

"Haunted?" I finished the sentence for him. "Yeah, that's what I'm saying. And I think it's all connected."

I couldn't deny the feeling that the two events—Cordelia's death and the missing body—were somehow tied together. I knew it sounded ludicrous, two events over a hundred years apart being linked. But Cordelia's warning was making a believer out of me.

An evil presence lurked in this very dwelling where we stood. A terror had stalked Cordelia and the rest of the Bloodson family. She clearly had been frightened for her life, and something she had seen, something she had felt, had been after her. I continued reading as the messages coalesced in front of me:

...he seems unwell...
...a strange fury is brooding inside him...
...an omen as the nightmares have come to life...
...I fear I may not be here much longer...

And most chilling of all:

Some days I feel a subliminal wrath...a curse is set against us, set on destroying...

The curse wasn't merely the stuff of legend. It was real. Documented in this very diary. And most curious of all: it preexisted Reginald's death.

Caution flashed inside me that everything I thought I knew, all the urban myths that had been passed down through the generations, were not in fact as they seemed. The secrets in these pages, Cordelia's hidden confessions, were about to alter history.

The Diary of Cordelia Bloodson

June 1, 1836

I have seen things I cannot explain. I realize it is lunacy to make such a declaration, but a specter is bent on killing me. It lives here, in our very home, and I have no way to escape it. I fear it is coming for me, and soon.

Reginald's disposition has concerned me for some time. The more I observe him, the more I come to realize that he seems unwell, as if a strange fury is brooding inside him. Yet he is not the only one beset by demons. Lately an apparition has appeared at my bedside, murmuring in my ear cunning lies, empty promises, vague auguries of things to come. I am robbed of precious sleep until the morning's wee hours, when at last I fall into troubled slumber...only to awaken with this harbinger of doom's whispers echoing in my fevered mind.

To occupy my idle hands, I have been continuing my experiments with plant hybridization. I have successfully crossbred two unique species through a series of grafting, a method I have been perfecting over the past year. I spoke of this grand achievement with my dear sister-in-law, but Gertrude seemed unimpressed. I've contented myself with adorning the dinner table with bouquets of this lovely hybrid, a nightly ritual poor Reginald, lost in his private torment, fails to appreciate.

I should not blame Gertrude for her apathy, as she has lost a child while I'm carrying my fifth. Her mood has grown dreary, yet she puts on a brave face as she tends to my every need as midwife.

In contrast to Gertrude's tender kindness, my own feelings have become cruel and irritable, and while I wish it to be simply a side effect of the brutal June heat, I sense it is something much more sinister at work. I fear I may not be here much longer, as some days I feel a subliminal wrath coursing its way through my family. Truly, a curse is set against us, bent on destroying our very lives. Yet my words go unheeded by all.

Or perhaps the curse is upon me alone.

Chapter 7

The last line I read hung in the stagnant air as we all remained speechless. What more was there to say, since Cordelia's premonition of impending doom had come true? I was left with more questions than answers, more doubts than ever.

I was about to make some lame quip to ease the tension when the thump returned with a vengeance. And then again, shaking the bones of the house. My flashlight flickered, then spookily enough gave up the ghost. We were cast into complete darkness.

A moment later Tara flicked hers back on, sweeping light across the hallway. I closed the diary and tucked it through the flannel shirtsleeves wrapped around my waist.

"What was that sound?" she asked.

"I keep hearing it, but I can't figure out where it's coming from. It sounds like somewhere downstairs."

"Before it was coming from the attic," Jonah reminded me.

"All I know is there's a reason they say to run from things that go bump in the night," Chris cut in, huddling close to the group. "Can we go now?"

I was just as ready to leave. "Yeah, let's head out before your batteries die too." I glanced at Tara, who clutched her flashlight like our lives depended on it. Considering what had happened here, perhaps they did.

As Jonah led the way down the second-story hall, a creak of wood stopped me mid-step. I grabbed Jonah's arm and yanked him to a stop, raising my finger to my lips for everyone to be quiet.

"Listen," I whispered.

Tap. Tap. Tap.

It wasn't the telltale creaking and groaning of a house settling—and God knows this old firetrap had plenty of time to settle! And it wasn't that loud thump reverberating inside the walls. It sounded more like…footsteps.

A moment later a door downstairs slammed shut. Chris and Jonah exchanged a wary look, then Tara and I did the same.

"Guys, what was that?" Jonah whispered.

"Sounded like the front door," Tara surmised.

I gulped. "But I propped it open…remember?"

"I told you this place was haunted!" Chris insisted with rising panic. "Why won't y'all listen to me?"

"Ghosts can't slam doors," I scoffed, sounding braver than I felt.

Either prospect wasn't good, whether it was a ghost or a person lurking late at night on the anniversary of—I mentally counted Cordelia, Reginald, his four sons, his fifth son, and the missing body—*eight* different deaths in

59

this very location. We practically tripped over each other on our way down the central staircase, all of us eager to get out as quickly—and alive—as possible. As I reached the bottom landing, Tara's flashlight went dark.

"Son of a bitch!" Chris swore. "Tara nearly broke her leg on a rotten board, we all hear spooky sounds we can't explain, my sister just happens to find a mysterious diary, the front door slams shut, and now our only working flashlight goes out. One horror movie cliché on top of another!"

Jonah managed a nervous chuckle. "Just wait, Leatherface will come out of a secret passage any second now and slice us to pieces with his chainsaw."

"You're as funny as a fart in Sunday school, Jonah," Chris muttered.

Tara yelled at the flashlight, banged it with the heel of her hand, flicked the switch back and forth, but it was no use.

"Guess we'll have to find our way through the woods in the dark, guys," I announced.

"Horror movie cliché number 452!" Chris moaned.

I glanced out one of the huge walk-through windows in the living room. Visibility was nearly nonexistent as the moon had again decided to play hide-and-seek behind a sky full of clouds. Amid the shadows casting strange shapes across the walls, I felt a presence hiding within them.

Reginald's ghost? Cordelia's? Or whoever's body had

been hanging from the rafters? There were plenty of dead people to pick from.

"C'mon. We've got to get out of here," I insisted, having heard enough disembodied sounds a la *The Haunting* to last me a lifetime.

I headed for the front door, which I only now realized was in fact closed.

"How did this swing shut?" I grumbled, pulling on the stuck doorknob. "Help me open this!"

"Where do you think you're going?" It was a voice not belonging to anyone in my group.

I pivoted around, watching a lanky form close in on us. Then another slid up behind it. Shrouded in black, I couldn't make out their features, only vague shapes, but there was one detail I was certain of as the moon peeked out just long enough to reveal.

One of them was holding a gun, and it was aimed directly at me.

Chapter 8

I figured ghosts didn't carry guns, so that left only crazed psycho-killers as the alternative. It wasn't a good one.

Panic gushed through me, working its way from my brain to my lungs, and I could barely breathe, let alone think. The only thing keeping me standing was adrenaline.

"Please," Tara begged of the figures, "we just want to go home!"

"Why are you here?" the same voice demanded, only this time I sensed a familiarity in it.

"We were just looking around," Jonah answered.

"You shouldn't be here," another voice warned.

Now this voice I *definitely* recognized. The nasal quality was unmistakable. And if it belonged to the person I thought it was, then he had some *'splainin' to do*.

"Leo—is that you?"

"Leo, as in *Leonard Valance*?" Jonah spat. Literally. I felt the spray of spit fly from his mouth, he was so angry. "You know this jerkwad?"

Leo Valance was a compact dude with the ultra-slim, wiry physique of a bronc buster, and taut muscles in all the right places. He looked more than a little like Luke Perry, with the same high forehead with expressive crinkles, same smirk, same hooded eyes, same great hair. In a word: he was dreamy.

"Who's asking? And what's it to you?" Now a very identifiable Victor, Leo's older brother, stepped forward into a patch of fleeting moonlight and lowered the barrel of the gun.

I exhaled the anxiety attack that had nearly suffocated me and made me braindead.

Pulling out a cigarette, Leo lit it up and walked past his brother. He was standing barely a foot away from me now. "Peace Christie, is that you?"

Leo Valance and I had kind of an on-again, off-again romantic history. With our feuding families being the Montagues and Capulets of Bloodson Bay, it was more off than on, I guess.

"Yeah, it's me. What are you guys doing here? And why are you carrying a gun?"

"It's a BB gun," Vic answered, "in case we came across any coyotes. You know the woods are full of 'em, don't you?"

Jonah snorted. "Just like a redneck—brings a BB gun to a coyote fight. You can't take a coyote down with a BB, dickweed."

Vic balled his fist and took a step toward Jonah. Leo threw his arm out to stop him.

"We know that," Leo said, blowing out a puff of smoke. "It's just to scare them off."

63

"We're not scared of coyotes. Or anything else." Jonah puffed out his chest, as if he hadn't almost peed himself a minute ago.

"You should be scared, if you had any brains," Vic cut in. "Especially considering all the shit that's gone down here."

I didn't want to hear another word about the horrors of the Slaughter Shed as we stood here surrounded by darkness with no working flashlights, strange sounds in the walls, and a dead body that went AWOL. All I wanted to do was curl up in my bed with Fiona Apple on my Discman singing me to sleep.

Pushing through the crowd of kids, I headed for the door. The umbrella stand I'd placed in front of it was toppled over on its side. At least no ghost had moved it.

"Okay, which one of you dipsticks slammed the door?" I demanded of the Valance brothers.

"I did," Vic spoke up. "Thought I'd give you punks a good scare."

"Too bad it didn't work," Jonah lied. It was obvious to everybody he was spoiling for a fight. Vic returned his *I hate your guts* scowl.

"Can someone help me open this?" The doorknob wiggled a little too loosely, and I worried about ripping it right out of the wood, leaving us trapped in here. I hadn't found another exit yet, and I wasn't eager to go searching for one in the dark.

Handing his cigarette to Vic, Leo appeared at my side.

I'd forgotten how good he smelled: a musky medley of hay, loam, and honest sweat, with a jigger of Hugo Boss tossed in. "Here, you have to do it like this," he said, gently tugging and lifting while I nearly swooned.

Then I heard the most beautiful sound in the world as the door flung open. I rushed outside, trailed by Tara, Chris, then Jonah shooting Vic and Leo a death stare on his way out. The moon reappeared between a gap in the clouds, sprinkling silver beams all over a field of swaying grass and wildflowers that tickled my ankles as I made my way to the cliff's edge.

Along the jagged drop-off lay a huge boulder that memorialized the spot where Reginald had pushed his children into the bay below, then dove to his own death. I headed toward the rock, drawn to it. The sound of the sloshing sea below mesmerized me like a trance.

I bent over to search the rock's face, tracing each letter that had been carved into the stone over a century ago:

The blood of the innocent is on your hands.

The expression chilled me. Soon the words were flying off the rock, circling me like vultures, as if they were about to attack.

I closed my eyes, imagining that one step that would send me falling into the churning sea. Moonlight-blond hair swirling around me like a halo as I sunk into the watercolor depths beneath the waves. It felt so real, as if I was already drowning…

"Peace, what are you doing?" Chris screamed frantically, pulling me back.

I suddenly felt his voice skip right past my ears and enter my heart, accelerating its rhythm. Blinking myself back to the cliff, I realized I had been standing precariously close to the edge, the toes of my boots jutting off the crumbling earth. I stumbled back several steps to safety, gasping for breath. I had no recollection of walking there, no idea I had been one step from falling. What was it about this place that drove people to madness? Maybe after inhaling whatever black mold was growing in Bloodson Manor, the veil between dream and reality had been slashed to ribbons.

Five sets of eyes stared at me in shock. I quickly traded my terrified expression for an embarrassed grin. Tara's mouth hung open. Chris looked at me like I belonged in a mental ward. And Jonah's eyes teared up with…what, I wasn't sure.

"Peace…" The way Jonah said my name, I heard what he was feeling. It sounded an awful lot like love.

"What the hell was that?" Vic demanded, asking the question on everybody's mind.

"I don't know," I muttered, still in shock. "I guess I kind of zoned out for a minute."

Tossing the cigarette on the ground, Vic put it out with the toe of his boot. His thumb was hooked in a belt loop of his Levi's beside a gaudy, oversized belt buckle with a custom V emblazoned on it. A proud proclamation of the wealth and power the Valance family held over Bloodson Bay. As the richest family in town who owned the most land and the biggest horse ranch, they were our family's primary competition—both personally and professionally. A feud that dated back over a century kept us bitter enemies, and our competing horse ranches made us constant rivals.

The Valances tried to outbid us on most of the horses that came through the kill pens—and they kept the healthiest, most well-trained horses for themselves while selling the rest to slaughterhouses that made dog food. We saved as many as we could, but our financial reach sometimes wasn't enough.

"Zoned out, hell," said Vic. "You was fixin' to join the rest of your crazy family at the bottom of the ocean as fish food!"

"Don't talk to my sister that way!" Chris came to my defense. "Or I'll turn *you* into fish food!"

We all knew it was an empty threat, as Vic and Leo stood a whole foot taller than Chris, and they had already developed man muscles where Chris was still just a scraggly skin-and-bones boy.

"All of you knock it off!" Tara chimed in. "You never told us what you're doing here—on private property, by the way." She glanced challengingly at Vic, then Leo.

"It's none of your business," Vic shot back. He softened his tone, smiled, and added, "Sorry, didn't mean to snap at you, darlin'. But really, Tara, you know you're too good for them. Why do you bother wasting your time with these losers?"

"You're calling us losers?" Chris sneered. "You're one to talk. At least my dad didn't send his own brother to prison!"

I remembered when the article had appeared in the *Bloodson Bay Bulletin*—with the story being heavily embroidered by the town gossips. Judge Ewan Valance sentenced his own brother, Marv, to jail for drug possession and dealing. Needless to say, it didn't look good for their family, though Judge Valance turned it into a publicity stunt proving his fidelity to the law, even when faced with a personal conflict of interest.

The scent of rain filled my nostrils, and I turned my attention to the sky. Low clouds scudded above the watery horizon, and out in the distance a squall twisted like a... rope, I thought morbidly.

"Everyone, shut up! I think a storm's coming," I said. But no one was paying me any mind. They were all preoccupied with a ridiculous male rivalry.

"You're trespassing on our property, so you better explain yourselves," Chris jumped in.

"Oh, feeling threatened that I'm going to steal your crush? Don't worry, dude, you can't lose something you never had in the first place."

"Enough already with the pissing contest! Were you following us?" I demanded.

It was no secret that our families had hated each other for as long as I could remember, though over what, I had never really understood. Our parents refused to explain why, and I had never given it much thought...until Leo came along.

"I swear, Peace, I wasn't behind it—" Leo stammered.

"Behind what?" I wanted to know.

A flash of lightning sizzled the air, giving me a full view of Leo...and the glint of metal around his neck.

"Nothing!" Then Vic turned to Leo. "And you need to shut your trap."

"Hey, you better start talking, or it's gonna be on like Donkey Kong." Jonah raised his fists, setting his feet in a boxing stance.

Vic sized Jonah up. "Shee-it, are you challenging me to a fight, punk?" he jeered. "I'll kick your face so far up your ass you'll be burping farts."

He elbowed Leo in the ribs, and the brothers fell all over each other laughing.

That was the opening Jonah was waiting for. His fist smashed against Vic's chin, knocking him into Leo. Vic vaulted back, swinging a furious right. Jonah ducked and came up with a head-butt into Vic's belly. A painful whoosh escaped Vic's lungs as he toppled over on his back, flailing his arms and legs like an upended turtle. Jonah leapt aboard Vic's chest and was using his face for a punching bag when Tara screamed, "Jonah, stop! You're killing him!"

"That's the idea," Jonah hissed, not letting up for a second.

"Hey, man, chill!" Leo yelled, pulling Jonah off his brother so Chris and I could hold him back. Jonah shook us off and shoved Leo in the chest.

"You lay your hands on me again, Leo, and you're dead meat."

Leo regarded Jonah with grudging respect. "Whatever you say, Rocky," he smirked.

Vic had clambered to his feet and stood rubbing his jaw. Tara went over to him and gingerly placed her hand on his arm.

"Are you all right, Vic?"

Vic smiled at her. "Yeah, I'm fine, darlin'."

Next to me, Chris seethed with jealousy. I could hardly blame him.

Vic turned to Jonah. "Low blow, punk, knocking the wind out of me," he said. "I'll kick your ass next time."

Jonah's eyes still blazed. "Why wait?"

He was about to pounce again when I grabbed his arm. He backed down, and I could practically see the excess testosterone drain from his body at my touch. He looked at me and grinned.

"Saved by your girlfriend," Vic taunted. "Come on, Leo, let's go. The air around here stinks. Later, freaks."

It should have ended there, as the Valance brothers turned to leave, but Vic couldn't resist taking a parting jab. "You all deserve to join your fruit loop kinfolk in the same gruesome death," he said, spinning around and pointing his finger directly at me. "You're just like them."

"*Just like them?*" I repeated. "What's that supposed to mean?"

"Don't you know what *really* happened?" He scrutinized me, then Chris. "Oh, wow, you don't know. You've believed a lie all this time. There's a reason our family hated yours for over a century—and a *good* reason."

"Vic, stop!" Leo hushed him.

A boom of thunder silenced them all, followed by a strange reverberation that ran up my feet, into my legs, filling my body. For a moment I thought it was only me, until Tara spoke up.

"Do you feel that?"

"It's just thunder," Jonah reasoned.

"No, I can feel it too," Chris said.

"Oh, crap." Vic looked at Leo. "Run!"

Run they did. And as they hightailed it through the woods, I stole one last longing glance at Leo's perfect butt.

By now the rumbling was shaking the ground, scattering tiny pebbles off the side of the cliff. North Carolina wasn't on any fault line that I knew of, so it couldn't be an earthquake. But the tremor grew louder, more intense with every second. Either Bloodson Manor was telling us in no uncertain terms to scram, or something very terrible was about to happen.

Chapter 9

As I waved Tara, Chris, and Jonah to follow me toward the woods, my absolute worst-case scenario had arrived, the one I feared most. The one I spent every day avoiding, dedicated endless hours to preventing. And yet it was here.

The rumble was no longer a low tremble but a deafening grumble. I recognized the rippling of earth, the rhythmic beat closing in on us. And I had no idea how to stop it.

"What is that sound?" Jonah turned to me.

"I think it's a—" I fumbled for the word.

Before I could finish the thought, Chris screamed to our scattered group, "Stampede! It's the horses! We have to stop them!"

Chris pointed across the field, toward a wall of trees. Emerging from the wood line was Thor, our newest rescue horse, who had no familiarity with the property and had built no trust with me yet.

His head bobbed back and force as he galloped, chest heaving, leg muscles swelling with each step. Behind him a herd of a couple dozen horses followed in a brash charge. Where the meadow dropped off the headland wasn't even a football field wide, which gave me very little time to react, let alone divert the horses to safety…without scaring them over the cliff or getting us trampled.

Another crack of lightning sent Thor rearing in terror, and the peal of thunder only escalated their speed. The storm was feverishly working against us. A singular thought flashed through my mind, the words inscribed on the stone memorial:

The blood of the innocent is on your hands.

It came down to two choices, both a huge gamble. One would guarantee my friends' safety, but the horses would likely plummet off the cliff. The other option could save the horses but get us trampled to death. It wasn't a light decision, but I knew myself. I knew Chris. And I knew my friends.

We couldn't let the horses die. I spent my entire life saving them from certain death; I wasn't about to let them self-destruct that easily. If there was ever a time to earn Thor's trust, it was now.

A steady rain was falling now, hampering our visibility. As if the situation weren't bad enough, Tara was in hysterics, sobbing uncontrollably.

"What do we do?" she bawled. "We've got to do some—"

"Get a grip, Tara! I've got an idea, but you guys are going to have to trust me. Come on!"

Waving Tara, Chris, and Jonah to follow me, I ran for the cliff's edge and scrambled directly in the path where the horses were steadily approaching.

"We've got to get in front of them to reroute them."

"Heeeeellllll no, I'm not jumping in front of a bunch of crazed horses!" Jonah protested, backing away.

"Please, Jonah, it's the only way to stop them!" I begged, hoping I didn't regret this idea and get us all killed.

"Hold your arms out like this and sing Fiona Apple's song 'Criminal,'" I explained, demonstrating by stretching my arms out.

Chris did a double-take. "You want us to sing? You're kidding, right?"

The horses were nearly on top of us, rounding the bend in a thundering knot.

"No, I'm not kidding! I sing that when I'm cleaning their stalls. If we sing loud enough, I think they'll hear us know it's me and calm down. We have to at least try."

"To hell with that shit!"

To our wondering eyes Chris got a running start, vaulted off a loblolly pine stump, and managed to grab hold of the halter of the lead horse, a three-year-old mare. He hung there for two Mississippis, his feet kicking frantically against her flank as he hoisted himself up on her back. I saw his strong legs tighten around her belly, and with both hands clutching the mane, he bent down over her neck and seized her right ear in his teeth!

I thought my little brother was crazy, but as I looked on in disbelief, she slowed to a canter, then a trot, down to a walk. Behind her, the other horses quickly followed suit—and just in time. Foam beaded upon their heaving bodies from their exhausting run. They were still a little restive, milling about and whinnying, but at least they'd been spared the Bloodson curse and hadn't plunged over the cliff—and maybe taking us with them.

And to think my goober of a little brother was the hero. I could hardly believe it.

I watched as Chris threw his legs over the horse's side and dropped to the ground. Jonah and Tara ran over to him and smothered him in congratulations.

"Damn, dude, that was the most amazing thing I've ever seen!" Jonah gushed. "Tom Cruise, eat your heart out!"

"I knew you'd been in rodeos," whispered an awestruck Tara, caressing his arm, "but like…triple wow!"

Clearing eating up the attention, Chris affected an aw-shucks demeanor. "Ah, just something I saw in a John Wayne movie once."

I guess I shouldn't have been surprised at Chris's heroics—he'd performed equally brave and impressive feats in rodeos, after all—but damned if I wasn't a little bit jealous.

"When you're through patting yourself on the back," I cut in, "would you mind telling me why in the hell you left the pasture gate open?"

Leaving a gate open was a rookie mistake, a lesson that had been drilled into us since before we could walk. It was a nasty and petty accusation, and Chris didn't take kindly to it. He stormed up to me, snarling, "Are you out of your frigging mind? I double-checked it, like I always do."

"Well, someone must have either left it open or the horses broke through the fence." I made a mental note to check the fence line when we got home before putting the horses to pasture.

I grabbed hold of two older horses' halters, calming them with soothing words and nose nuzzles. I had had enough adventure for one day, I decided, as I led the horses toward where we had come in. The herd seemed eager to follow and formed a trail behind me while Chris grabbed two more.

It was a long, grueling process leading the herd back to the farm, with several stopping to graze and others wandering off the path. While Chris walked beside me, Tara and Jonah hung at the rear. Despite a few minor setbacks, we managed to make it through the woods in the dark and back to the barn at the bottom of a hill from our house. Sure enough, the pasture gate hung wide open, and I resolved to find out who to blame come morning. It wasn't a mistake you could make twice.

I watched Chris guide the horses into the pasture, feeling bad for him and his fragile ego. Considering the distance he had put between himself and Tara on the way back, it was obvious he was embarrassed by what Victor had said to him back at Bloodson Manor: *You can't lose something you never had in the first place.* I knew my brother adored Tara, and it wasn't really clear if she reciprocated his feelings.

After securing the horses and checking the fence—I was paranoid by this point that they'd escape again—I did a head count and realized we were missing one. It took three more headcounts before I figured out who wasn't accounted for.

"Guys, Thor's missing. We need to go out and look for him." I was soaked and sapped and sleepy. All I wanted to do was fall into bed, but I couldn't leave Thor out there wandering around in a storm.

Grabbing an extra flashlight from the barn, we headed across the field back the way we had come. Back to that condemned Bloodson Manor that was quickly becoming the bane of my existence. At least the weather had an ounce of mercy for us as the rain thinned to a mist.

While Jonah, Tara, and I walked together—with Chris dejectedly hanging back a few steps—calling out for Thor, I remembered what Victor had said about our family *believing a lie all this time.*

"What lie do you think Vic was talking about?" I speculated aloud.

"You can't trust anything the Valance brothers say. Their whole family is a bunch of liars," Tara answered.

"Of course you'd say that. You know Vic likes you," Chris replied grumpily a beat behind us.

"Oh, stop it. He does not. And even if he did, it's not like I like him back."

"You sure about that?" Chris sounded wounded, but I wanted to slap some sense into him. "Because it sure looked like you did."

"Whatever. Think what you want. I don't need to defend myself to you. I'm going to check over here for Thor." Then Tara disappeared into the woods.

I knew Chris hated the Valances almost as much as I pretended to, but it seemed like a pointless rivalry. I had long suspected that our parents had withheld the truth from us, but now I was determined to find out what exactly the truth was. I just had to make sure my own secrets didn't slip out in the process. Reginald's secrets had destroyed our family once; I couldn't let history repeat itself with me.

"Hey, I found Thor!" Tara's voice wasn't too far off, thank God. "I'm holding his halter, but I'll need you to come get him. We're over here near the graveyard."

The graveyard? I didn't know about any graveyard. And I wasn't sure I wanted to be near one after the crazy, spooky night we'd had.

As I followed Tara's voice, my flashlight guiding me, the woods opened up into a small square clearing. A crumbling stone wall surrounded the back and sides about waist high, and a rusted wrought iron fence ran across the front. A tiny gate hung crookedly from the middle of the fence.

Inside the overgrown graveyard, moss-covered stones

jutted up from the damp earth in a short row, partially hidden by tufts of grass and years of fallen leaves. Stepping further inside the clearing, I realized what I was standing in.

Our family plot.

I wiped a leaf off the name on the first stone, the letters in the slick gray marble worn shallow over time, but still legible:

Reginald Bloodson

Moving across the row to the next grave, I read the second name:

Cordelia Bloodson

Further along were four more names, each one of their four sons that Reginald had thrown from the cliff, as the death dates all matched Reginald's: June 27, 1837.

As I read the next three tombstones, goosebumps sprouted all over my body. Suddenly so much more made sense. A horrible, terrible sense.

Chapter 10

Dr. Edgar Valance
Gertrude Bloodson-Valance
Genevieve Valance

Three marble headstones, as ancient as time, with three names that told a whole new history. As I examined the weathered names, passing my flashlight over the details of their births and deaths, a story formed in my mind. A story that explained a family rivalry that was powerful enough to be passed down from generation to generation.

Once upon a time there were two friends. Friends closer than brothers. Reginald Bloodson and Dr. Edgar Valance. Then one day something destroyed their friendship, twisting them into mortal enemies. But what force was strong enough to destroy brotherhood?

Love.

It was always love.

As I mentally connected the dots, I came to my own conclusion. Reginald and Edgar had been close enough friends at one point that Reginald's sister, Gertrude *Bloodson-Valance*, had married into the Valance family.

Edgar was even buried in the Bloodson family plot. But what caused the rift? It had to be love.

Perhaps Reginald didn't condone Edgar's marriage to his sister, or maybe Edgar treated Gertrude poorly. Whatever the case, the Valances had at one point been family, connected by marriage. Love. But something along history had broken that bond irreparably. If I traced it back far enough, dug deep enough, I wondered if I could find out what caused the rift.

The third headstone, that of Genevieve Valance, was smaller than the other two, and the birth and death dates listed revealed she had been months old when she died. An infant grave. So terribly heartbreaking.

I could only assume the rift happened shortly after Dr. Edgar Valance's death, as no one else in the Valance family was buried here. I guessed they were buried in the Bloodson Bay Cemetery, where most of the town's citizens were buried.

"Do you think this has something to do with what Vic was talking about—some lie about the past?" Chris gestured to Edgar's tombstone.

Maybe my logic wasn't so far-fetched after all if even my dimwitted brother wondered the same thing.

"I don't know, but I think I'll find some answers in Cordelia's diary." Excitement at the prospect of uncovering some big mystery coursed through me, overriding the bone-deep exhaustion. "I remember reading Gertrude's name in it. It sounded like she and Cordelia were close. Her secrets might be the key to unraveling this."

The diary! I patted the now empty spot where I had tucked it between the shirt wrapped around my waist.

"No!" I moaned, on the verge of tears. "The diary must have fallen out during the stampede. It's going to get ruined in this weather. I've got to go back and look for it."

"Peace, it's too late," Jonah said.

"I need to try! After everything we just went through..." I was so worked up that I couldn't hold the overwhelm in anymore. So I cried. Like a lost little girl, which was exactly how I felt. After spending my entire youth feeling like I had no purpose, I had finally felt destiny's pull. And that diary was the reason for it. "You don't understand. I *have* to go back."

"No you don't."

"Yes I do!" I screamed.

"Not if it's not there." I looked at Jonah quizzically as he pulled something out of his huge pants pocket and handed it to me. Cordelia's diary, in all its worn leather glory.

"I knew there was a reason you wore those hideous pants!" I squealed and hugged the breath out of him.

I couldn't wait to dig in. Sitting on the short stone wall surrounding the tiny cemetery, I opened the book up, flipping through to an entry bookmarked with a folded piece of paper.

"What's that?" Jonah asked over my shoulder.

I unfolded the page, finding a sketch of a man. At the bottom was the same signature we had seen on the portrait in the attic. Gertrude Bloodson. Quite the artistic talent.

"It looks like a sketch Gertrude drew."

"Wow, she was good," Jonah breathed into my ear. "Any idea who the drawing is of?"

I turned the page over and saw the name *Doctor Edgar Valance* written along the top, followed by the year 1836.

"It's her husband, Edgar," I answered.

Tara led Thor up behind me, and I could feel his lips searching along my neck for food. The horses often mistook my blonde hair for hay.

"He's actually kind of handsome," Tara commented.

"For an old dude," Chris grudgingly agreed.

Tara was right—I saw a strong resemblance to Leonard in the broody eyes, the bad-boy smirk, the high, intelligent brow...

"Peace, you still with us?" Tara shattered my unbidden reverie with a chuckle.

I blinked back to the cemetery, where Jonah eyed me suspiciously.

"Oh, yeah, sorry. I just got distracted for a moment." With fantasies of Leonard Valance.

Folding the sketch back up, I slid it between a couple pages in the front and returned to the entry I had found. Surrounded by Chris sitting on one side of me, Jonah's warm thigh pressed to mine on the other side, Tara looking over my shoulder, and Thor nibbling the collar of my T-shirt under my dress, I began to read out loud.

The sky was thinning to a concrete gray as dawn slowly approached. With each sentence we slowly slipped into the world back before the feud, back to Bloodson Bay in June of 1836…

The Diary of Cordelia Bloodson

June 13, 1836

A quarrel between Reginald and Doctor Valance awoke me in the early dawn, before the sun crested the horizon. I know not what they argue over, yet I have a suspicion.

I must confess my sins to you, dear diary, for I have no other confidante while forced to remain bedridden for the duration of my pregnancy. Succumbing to bored curiosity, I found something hidden in Gertrude's handbag that gave me cause for worry. Daily her heart breaks more for the baby she lost and the torturous infertility "remedies" inflicted on her by her husband. A sister closer than a friend, as I am, can sense such pain plaguing her. Perhaps her husband, the good doctor, can help her better than friendship can, though I feel he only makes it worse. She wears her pain with a smile, and I envy her strength.

I console Gertrude with conversation about my love for

horticulture, for which she seems to have developed a fondness Only she can understand the passions we women possess that men, in their arrogance, dismiss as frivolous.

I explained to her the medicinal properties of the various plant species, such as the antipyretic nature of Willow Bark that can subdue a fever, or the cathartic elements of herbs like Bloodroot that cleanse the bowels. She even offered to test a Belladonna hybrid that aids in sleep. So impressed was Gertrude in my work that she drew detailed pictures of each hybrid plant specimen for my records. Perhaps one day her artistry will be recognized for its great worth and my horticulture discoveries can advance the science of medicine.

My plants can only distract me so much. The mysteries surrounding this house only seem to be worsening as of late, so much that I fear for my life. Apparitions. Nightmares. Thus I hid Reginald's shaving razor in my steamer trunk at the foot of my bed for protection, and hid the key in my locket. He raved about his missing razor this morning while I assured him it would turn up eventually. God save me for the other secret I have hidden from my husband, tucked in a secret compartment under the false bottom of the chest for safekeeping, to be used only in case of emergency. I pray Reginald never finds it, or the end will surely come.

I must remind myself that although the grief of my sins

piles up with each lie, it is only out of necessity.

Footsteps draw near. For now I must return you to the compartment I constructed within the linen chute, lest my secrets unravel before unwanted eyes and condemn us all.

Chapter 11

I fell asleep that night imagining Cordelia's life.

The suffocating June heat trapped in her bedroom, withholding even the slightest breeze. A collection of hand-picked wildflowers scattered on her bedside table, their unique properties a fascinating distraction. Her pregnant belly jutting up from under her thin nightgown. The intoxicating scent of sweaty bedsheets crumpled at her bare feet in the very bed I had seen with my own two eyes at Bloodson Manor where she had bled out.

I woke up the next morning haunted by Cordelia's death. My body felt restless as I threw on jeans and a T-shirt to do barn chores in. My neck was stiff. My brain was overloaded. My nerves were zapped. The coffer that Cordelia described sounded like the one I had seen in the attic at Bloodson Manor. Something important was in that chest.

And I could feel it pulling me back to the Slaughter Shed.

The morning held a beautiful calm that only followed a wild storm. Perhaps the weather was as exhausted as I felt, blustering the last of its fury in the night and reenergized by a vibrant dawning sun.

I rushed through mucking stalls and feeding the horses, which proved to be a grave mistake when my arms felt like wet noodles afterwards. Microwaving a Pizza Pocket for lunch, I took it with me while I headed into the woods alone.

This was between me and Cordelia.

It took me half the time to find Bloodson Manor in the light of day compared to last night. The path to the overlook had been trampled down by the herd of horses, making it easier to find the way. When I arrived at the house, it looked nothing like it had in the dark. No sinister shadows. No eerie sounds. Instead I found it to be beautifully baroque, while still projecting a homey charm. Once upon a time this house had been a showplace, and perhaps could be again, with a little—okay, *a lot*—of TLC. But that was a project for Bob Vila, not someone who was all thumbs like me. I imagined four little boys playing on the double-decker porches while the large windows let in the cool evening coastal breeze.

My gaze traveled up the front of the house, settling on the third floor where I located the small attic window. A movement, a strange shadow that briefly resembled the shape of a head, passed behind the glass, then disappeared. I stared harder but saw nothing. A trick of the eye. It had to be. There were no signs of life here.

I climbed the porch steps, careful to avoid the broken step that Tara had fallen through. This time the front door swung easily open, revealing the innards in a whole new light.

The house was huge and palatial, despite evidence of vermin, peeling wallpaper, water stains, and sagging ceiling beams. Even in its rundown glory, the vast interior retained its sumptuous character. Once upon a time the Bloodsons clearly had money as I noted the details of the floating staircase and the flowers carved into the banisters. Such a shame that the place ended up forlorn like this. Cobwebs hung like tattered curtains, and dust covered every surface like a blanket.

I mounted the staircase slowly, taking in every detail as I ran my fingers along the glossy wood, noting the rich color and intricate petals. I rushed past Cordelia's bedroom, eager to avoid another glance at the place where she died.

At the end of the second-story hallway I found the small door that led up to the attic. While the rest of the house was open and bright, this stairwell was engulfed in darkness, with little natural light to guide me. At the top of the stairs I could see the faint glimmer of sun dappling the walls through the tiny window.

The top of the stairs opened up into a small, cluttered room—much more cluttered than I remembered—with a low vaulted ceiling. It was a tight space, forcing me to hunch; I felt like Alice, having unwisely sampled a magic drink and grown enormous, becoming stuck in the White Rabbit's house. Mindful of banging my head and knees as

I navigated the space, I prayed I wouldn't suffer a similar fate. The portrait that had so frightened me last night seemed benign enough now, but the man's smile, dripping with corruption and menace, was still disturbing.

A full view of the space offered so much more to explore. Sitting on a small table was a sketchbook filled with drawings. I opened it and flipped through, finding countless illustrations of plants and ocean views, some sketched in chalk, others in graphite. Closing it, I continued wandering around the room.

I almost forgot about the locket in the jewelry box, and the intriguing folded paper it contained, so I made a beeline for the table. I'd been kicking myself for not pocketing the trinket when I had the chance; that letter, or whatever it was, could be a vital clue. Rummaging through the box, the locket was nowhere to be found. I was *sure* I'd placed it back in the box before Jonah distracted me.

Curiouser and curiouser! cried Alice.

I noticed a miniature door built into the wall at the very back. That had to be the linen chute, its gaping throat leading to a laundry room I hadn't yet discovered. I opened the door, first noticing a pulley attached above it, then how much wider it was than our chute at home. I remembered one our countless family trips to historic towns along the East Coast, as Mom excitedly pointed out multipurpose ingenuity used in older homes. This looked fairly similar to a dumbwaiter that also served as a linen chute in one of the historic home tours.

91

Moving along, I found the spot where I thought the chest had been...but it was no longer there. I wandered the room, the muscles in my neck starting to ache from hunching over, unable to find it. Had I been that disoriented in the dark? I returned to the vacant spot, and in its place was a large empty rectangle where it had been, the dust that had surrounded it perfectly preserved as if it had simply been lifted up and moved.

I hadn't mentioned the chest to anyone outside of our group last night. So who knew about it? And more importantly, where was it?

Or maybe most important of all, why would someone take it?

Chapter 12

My mom, Elizabeth Christie, known by friends as Liz, wasn't like most moms. She wasn't the best cook. Or the best housekeeper. She burned mac 'n' cheese and rarely vacuumed. She worked too many long hours as the director of the Loving Arms Children's Home, and she wanted to rescue every child and animal in need. She stood on the opposite end of the political spectrum from my dad (Mom being a lifelong Democrat who loved Bill Clinton, warts and all, and Dad a dyed-in-the wool disciple of Ronald Reagan; oh, the debates they had!), but she steadfastly supported his mayoral candidacy and cheered louder than anyone when he won. And when it came to our family's background, she was a bona fide historian who knew too many random details that most people found boring but I found fascinating. So when I had no one else to turn to about Cordelia's missing trunk, Mom was the first, maybe only, person I could think who might help me find it.

After scribbling something down on a piece of paper, I folded and tucked it into my back pocket for later and went in search of Mom. I spotted her on the back porch sipping coffee, always bitter and black, while reading the

Bloodson Bay Bulletin. She was engrossed in an article about welfare reform law.

She must have sensed my presence because she set the newspaper down, revealing the front-page headline that read:

TIMOTHY MCVEIGH FOUND GUILTY OF OKLAHOMA CITY BOMBING

Below that article was another one, with a picture of a smiling teenage girl, braces on her teeth and hair chopped short. Upside down, she almost looked like...

"Oh my gosh. I know that girl! That's Emory McAlister. We've been classmates since kindergarten. She got a full scholarship to MIT."

I slid the newspaper toward me and flipped it around to read the headline:

LOCAL MISSING TEEN BELIEVED TO BE RUNAWAY

I couldn't imagine why anyone like Emory would run away when she was getting a full ride to her dream college. But then again, Emory had always been a rebel. Pink hair. Goth clothes. Unassumingly brilliant. Tech-savvy. An outspoken student and community activist not afraid to speak truth to power—no matter who they were. And that included folks like Judge Valance, who she'd taken to task at public forums, in guest editorials in the *Bulletin* (one of the few institutions the judge's influence hadn't tainted), and most especially in her hard-hitting personal weblog— no surprise, Emory she was a pioneer in that fairly new medium.

Emory was who I wished I could be. When I wasn't hating on her for being so much cooler than me, I was wanting to *be* her.

The more I thought about it, running away just didn't make sense for a girl like Emory who had everything going for her. What if her outspokenness had finally angered someone enough that they'd want to shut her up? And who might that someone be? Oh, I dunno... Yes, I did: Judge Valance. If anyone would want her out of the picture during his reelection campaign, it was that despicable fat cat.

"I'm so sorry, Peace. Was she your friend?" Mom asked.

"Not really. We hung out in different circles. But I just hope she's okay. The future needs more people like her."

And fewer corny people like me.

"Are you okay?" Mom knitted her brows; a wan smile died on her face.

Was the guilt over the secret I kept from her written across my forehead?

"Yeah, I'm fine. Why?"

"You just look...stressed, that's all."

Stressed—who, me? No way was I stressing over my hoard of lies, Jonah's unreciprocated crush on me, the grudge against the Valances, the terrifying horse stampede, and a house that seemed determined to kill me.

"I didn't get much sleep last night. Someone left the horse gate open and it took forever rounding them up."

Mom's lips parted with an impending barrage of questions I had already anticipated.

"Don't worry, Mom—I got them all back in and did a head count half a dozen times. Everyone's safe."

"And the gate—is it secure?"

"Yeah. I still don't know who left it open, though. Uncle Bernie seemed pretty drunk last night. Maybe he left the gate open without realizing it. I'll mention it to him tactfully."

"Good idea, honey. Why don't you take the rest of the day off from chores and relax? It's a gorgeous day. Go do something fun with your friends."

I found it oddly pathetic that my *friends* Mom referred to were my brother and *his* friends. One of them being a guy who had an unrequited crush on me. But she was right. The sun wasn't too harsh, the breeze was inviting, and a trail ride could be the perfect salve for what ailed me. Nature and animals offered a therapy nothing else compared to.

"Can I ask you something real quick?" I pulled out the piece of paper from my pocket and unfolded it, handing it to her. "Do you know anything about a chest that looks like this?" I had drawn a sketch of it, giving extra attention to the ornate lock that had stood out to me.

Mom held the picture, examining it carefully as a gust of wind tugged at it.

"Where did you see this steamer trunk? This is the Bloodson coat of arms on this lock here." She pointed to the crown on one side of the lock. "This crown signifies Reginald's forefather's name, whom he was named after, which means *king*." Then she moved her finger to the other side, pointing to a sword. "And this is because the Bloodsons were known for being warriors...hence the surname."

I told Mom about our exploration of Bloodson Manor last night—omitting the missing body and bloodstains on the floor, of course—and described how I had found the chest in the attic but it was gone this morning. Like the cool mom that she was, she didn't get all bent out of shape. But I was pretty sure we weren't allowed to venture out near the *death cliff*, as my parents called it. I hated to lie to her, but what she didn't know wouldn't hurt her.

"It's been ages since I've checked out the back of the property. How did the house look?"

"Like it's been abandoned for 160 years," I answered.

"I really need to get back there and clear that place out and salvage what we can. I've been wanting to restore the house, or at least the furniture inside. I hate that it's all rotting away. As for that chest, I have no idea where it could have gone. No one ever goes back there, so my guess is a bunch of kids must have been trespassing and took it."

One set of trespassers came to mind, and that was the

Valance brothers, who happened to have been there last night. The timeline fit. And if they had no guilt over trespassing, I doubted a little theft would bother them.

"One more thing, Peace," Mom said, touching my wrist. "You should ask your Uncle Bernie about this. He could probably answer a lot of your questions about the family history and Bloodson Manor."

"What about Bloodson Manor?" Mom and I both turned to find Chris at the foot of the porch. Pieces of sandwich flew out of his mouth as he spoke while climbing the steps with Jonah tagging along.

When Chris wasn't sleeping or playing Nintendo, he was eating. Where all those calories went was anyone's guess.

Mom greeted Jonah, then answered, "We were just talking about something your sister found at the house last night. I thought your uncle might know a little more about it."

Then a thought occurred to me. I hadn't seen Chris all morning until now. Or Jonah or Tara, for that matter. Which was unusual, since they were always around.

"You guys didn't go back to the house earlier today, did you?" I asked Chris.

"No, why?"

"Remember that trunk we found in the attic, Jonah?"

"Yeah, what about it?"

"It's gone."

He shrugged disinterestedly. "Weird."

"Yeah, weird…" I replied. But Jonah's aloof response was weirder than the chest disappearing.

"Where's Tara?" Mom asked.

It was also weird for Chris and Jonah to be hanging out without Tara. Even though I often teased my brother about her being too cool to hang out with him, they were usually inseparable.

"I don't know," he replied matter-of-factly. "We're not obligated to spend every waking moment together just because we're friends."

And yet they always did. Something was up.

"Are you two still fighting? I thought you would have made up by now."

"What's it matter to you, Peace? She can do what she wants. It's not like she's my girlfriend."

"Jeez, Chris, just make up already," I mumbled.

"How? What am I supposed to say?"

"Just say you're sorry, stupid," Jonah wisely suggested. "Girls like to think they're right and you're wrong. As long as you let them believe it, you can do whatever you want."

So maybe it wasn't as wise as I thought. It *was* Jonah, after all, whose pants sagged halfway to his knees and who wouldn't recognize a bottle of shampoo if it dropped on his head.

"I'm pretty sure it's more complicated than that." Chris balled up the last square of his sandwich and hurled it at Jonah, then stomped inside through the back door, leaving me, Mom, and Jonah bewildered.

I looked at Jonah for an explanation of Chris's behavior, but he only shrugged. "Beats me."

"Well, I'm going to find my uncle to see if I can get some answers about the chest," I said.

Jonah didn't budge. Didn't blink. Just grinned sheepishly at me. I knew that look. He wanted an invitation.

"Do you want to come with me?" I finally offered.

"Heck yeah! Uncle Santa always offers me a beer when I stop by his place."

Mom gasped. "Excuse me? Bernie offers you *what?*"

"I'm just kiddin', Mrs. C." Not according to the wide-eyed guilt on Jonah's face.

As we headed down the porch steps and out into the sun, swollen and high in the sky, we walked until we rounded a stand of trees. There the face of Uncle Bernie's trailer—a stern gray—frowned at us with its lopsided porch and wilting steps.

"Hey." I grabbed Jonah's shoulder, stopping him mid-stride. "Leave the talking to me, okay?"

Chapter 13

Uncle Bernie's trailer was nestled in the far corner of the farm's property, giving him all the privacy he could want with all the accessibility he would need. As the ranch farmhand, we relied on him to do everything we couldn't do, or didn't have time to do. Which was pretty much anything and everything.

Replacing broken rails. Fixing stall doors. Mowing overgrown pastures. Rebuilding a rotted chicken coop. You name it, Uncle Bernie did it.

Standing on the small stoop he called a front porch, I knocked on the door, which rattled on its rusty hinges. When no one answered after a minute, I knocked again.

"Uncle Bernie!" I called out. "You home?"

This prompted a boom of bootsteps from inside the house clomping toward the door. It cracked open just wide enough for me to see Uncle Bernie's bulbous nose, crawling with spidery red gin blossoms, and florid cheeks gashed with sleep wrinkles.

"Tell your ma I already seeded the pasture and I'm taking a nap," he said, rubbing his eyes.

He was about to shut the door on me when I spoke up.

"No, it's not about work."

"Then whaddya want?"

"I was wondering if you knew about a steamer trunk left at Bloodson Manor. I found one there last night. It had the family crest on the lock. Do you know which one I'm talking about?"

"Nope."

His face betrayed a flicker of recognition. So I handed him the drawing I had shown my mom. "It looks like this."

Uncle Bernie yanked the door and stepped out onto the porch, where he stood blinking like a drunken owl in the sunshine. "Can't say I've seen anything like it," he said, rubbing his bearded jaw with pretend interest. "Why would I know anything about that?"

Why was he lying to me?

"Mom said you knew quite a bit about the family history. I thought maybe you had seen the chest at some point. It was in the attic last night, but this morning I went back and it's gone missing."

Uncle Bernie scampered back into his house like a possum retreating into a hollow log. He knew something about it alright.

"Strange, I'll give ya that. But I gotta ask why you're still snoopin' around that old place anyway. It's a death trap. The whole building is falling apart. You're liable to get hurt running around there. You woke me up for this horseshit?"

"Why are you being so mean?" Jonah interjected,

earning a scowl from both me and Uncle Bernie.

"No one's talking to you, kid." Uncle Bernie stabbed a calloused finger at Jonah. "All of y'all stay outta that house, got it? Now, get the hell outta here. You interrupted my nap and I'll never fall back asleep," he grumbled, then slammed the door in our faces.

"What bug crawled up his butt?" Jonah asked.

"I told you to keep your mouth shut," I stated pointedly.

It wasn't like Uncle Bernie to be short with me, and normally I would write it off as him having a bad day. But his reaction was too odd not to question it. We began walking across the field toward home when the rumble of Uncle Bernie's truck yanked my attention to his dirt and gravel driveway. The tires stirred up a cloud of red dust as they bumped along toward the main road into town.

"Hey, I thought he was napping..." I detected a thick note of suspicion in Jonah's voice. I glanced at him—yep, there was that *let's go find trouble* look.

"No, don't you even think it!" I warned.

"It sounds like you're thinking what I'm thinking." Cue the mischievous smirk I never trusted.

I took an educated guess at what he was thinking. "That we should break into his trailer and see what we can find?"

Jonah nodded, then dashed back toward the trailer before I could stop him. Though there was no stopping Jonah when he got an idea in his head, short of physically tackling him to the ground.

I was catching my breath by the time I joined him at the side of the house where he was peering through a shoulder-high window, testing each piece of glass along the wall.

"I think I know how we can get in." I waved Jonah to follow me to the rear.

I knew the spare bedroom window lock had been broken for ages and had never been fixed. Jonah gave me a leg up, and I shoved the window upward, easily sliding it open. Pulling myself inside, I fell arms-first onto the beige bedroom carpet, then was nearly trampled on by Jonah a minute later. Once inside, I glimpsed a whole new side of Uncle Bernie I'd never seen before.

A long white desk housed several computer screens, with huge computer towers next to each one.

"Holy crap," Jonah whispered in awe. "He's got over $8,000 worth of computer equipment in here. This trailer ain't even worth that much."

I scoffed. "Are you sure? How would Uncle Bernie even get that kind of money?"

"I'm telling you, I just saw a Best Buy ad for this Apple Macintosh selling for $2,500. I don't know how he's able to afford it as a farmhand unless your parents pay *really* well. I think I need to reconsider my career options."

Jonah continued walking down the line of computers, bending over to check out another one. "Hey, look, he has an old Commodore 64 over here."

I didn't know what that meant, and I doubted I would ever need to. Who even needed a computer when you had books and libraries? I was pretty sure computers were an overpriced fad that would die out just like the 8-track tape did.

Touching one of the mouses, I brought a screen to life showing rows and rows of green letters and numbers against a black background.

"Whoa, your uncle writes code?" Jonah asked, his stare fixed on the computer screen as he grabbed the mouse from me and scrolled down.

"Uhhh…is that supposed to be impressive? Because if so, I doubt he does."

Jonah seemed shocked at my response. "Heck yeah, it's impressive. You've never heard of C++ or DOS? You know, computer programming?"

"I've heard of it, but I don't know anything about it."

As if I would know what my uncle did with his computers. My only familiarity with them was the occasional internet research I did at the Bloodson Bay Library, or checking the email account I was forced to open when the family got a free internet trial disc in the mail from AOL. Dad had an Acer computer in his office, but no one was allowed to use it since we only had a limited number of internet hours that came with our free trial, and my parents were too cheap to purchase a monthly plan. Other than typing out a book report, what was the point of even having a computer?

"You can do all kinds of things with coding. Build a website, create video games, even hack into databases." Jonah was getting excited now. Apparently I had hit his sweet spot.

"You think my uncle—who can't even button his shirt up correctly—can write code?"

"Most computer geeks aren't worried about fashion, Peace. They're too busy holed up in their basements making bajillions of dollars creating dot-com companies that are going to pave the way to the future."

I laughed at his naiveté. "You think these stupid machines are the way of the future? No way. They're a pointless time suck, like video games, and just like kids outgrow video games, we'll outgrow computers too. Enough about the stupid computers. We're not here to fawn over codes. We're here to find some kind of clue to what my uncle knows about that chest."

Dragging Jonah away from the computers, we made our way quickly through each room in the house, finding nothing but dirty dishes, dirty clothes, and according to Jonah, dirty magazines. I had no desire to look at any of it.

"There's nothing here," Jonah said, giving up.

I gazed around the living room, searching for anything that seemed out of place. But everything seemed out of place. It was all useless junk, garbage.

Except for one thing.

On the windowsill sat an heirloom that used to belong to my grandmother. A priceless fancy little ceramic box decorated with birds in flight. Worth more than my life, Grandma had told me when I was a kid. It was at least a hundred years old back then, a fact she had screamed at me after I almost dropped it once. I was forbidden ever after from touching it again by the crotchety old cow.

So of course without Grandma here to scold me, I picked it up. I swung open the delicate lid, uncertain about what I was looking at.

"Jonah, check this out!"

A most unusual key was hugged by the red velvet interior, a tarnished key that looked to be as old as the ceramic box. Jonah reached inside just as I did; our hands pressed together, fingers skimming the velvet. He looked at me, and I looked at him. Our bodies were close, our shared gaze intimate. His eyes closed as he leaned forward awkwardly.

On instinct his lips parted, his mouth a subtle shift away. I was unaware I was leaning toward him until the first touch of our lips. The softness drew me in, igniting the living room on fire just long enough to warm my whole body, for me to forget where I was, what I was doing, who I was doing it with.

Suddenly I felt like someone had dumped ice water down my shirt.

My breath hitched, and I wrenched away. "What are you doing?"

But we both knew exactly what he was doing. What *we* were doing.

His eyelids popped open, wide and unblinking, and his cheeks reddened with mortification. Backing away from his unexpected—and most definitely unequivocally unwanted—kiss, the box fell to the floor with a sickening cracking sound, sending the key clattering across the floor. "No!" I screamed. I half expected my dead grandmother to hurl a lightning bolt at me from heaven...or to engulf me in flames from hell, more likely. "Jonah, look what you made me do!"

I hated to cast blame, but this was all his overeager mouth's fault.

Gingerly picking up the box, I examined it to see if it was salvageable. A cleft of missing ceramic from one corner, and a fissure down the side—at least it was on the back. Maybe if I superglued it together no one would know the difference.

"Go look in the kitchen junk drawers for any type of glue you can find."

I was furious at Jonah for his poor timing and even poorer judgment. What made him think kissing me in the middle of breaking and entering was *romantic*? I couldn't blame him, though. *Die Hard* was Jonah's idea of a rom-com.

Luckily every kitchen drawer was a junk drawer, because Jonah returned in record time with a tiny bottle of superglue. I untwisted the cap off and squirted a line up the ceramic crack, then pressed the pieces together, praying they'd adhere. I set the box back on the windowsill—

fractured side facing the window, of course—and told Jonah to put the superglue back.

He scooted back to the kitchen, then returned to the living room with a hangdog look on his face, as if I'd caught him whacking off to Uncle Bernie's girlie mags. I finally broke the pregnant silence.

"Hey, Jonah, are we going to talk about—" I wasn't sure how to end the question.

"The kiss?" he answered for me.

"Yeah, the kiss." I hadn't yet forgiven him for kissing me on the spot, but a subtle stirring, a hum inside me, hadn't exactly hated it either. Why were relationships so confusing? "It's just that we've been friends forever. You're like a brother to me."

Jonah winced. Apparently that was the worst possible thing I could have said. "You're right. Can't blame a guy for trying, though, can you? Let's just forget it ever happened and get out of here."

Right. Forget the kiss ever happened. The kiss that opened my eyes to a whole new side of Jonah I'd never noticed before. I could handle that.

On the way through the living room, I stepped on something hard. My heart sunk that I had just crushed another missing shard from the box that I hadn't noticed before, but when I lifted my foot, it was the key I had almost forgotten about.

I picked it up, cupping the cold metal in my warm palm. It was a very old key. The same crown and dagger

109

crest from the chest decorated its bow.

"Do you think this opens the chest?" I showed Jonah the matching end, holding it up to my drawing to compare the two. Even with my terrible artistic skills, they were a very close match.

"Probably. But we won't know until we find the chest." Jonah kept his distance from me, and I could tell he wanted to get as far away from me as humanly possible.

As he lingered halfway toward the computer room, the remnants of daylight faded to a yolky yellow. The sun seemed to sigh as it sank behind the trees. I was passing across the window when a rumble vibrated the glass and headlights slid across the wall behind me. I dropped down, ducking below the windowsill.

"He's home!" I whisper-yelled. "Go! Hurry!"

On Jonah's tail, I scrambled across the hallway just as Uncle Bernie's hand twisted the doorknob. I skirted around the doorway into the computer room just as the door opened. By the time Uncle Bernie's boots thumped down the hallway, my legs were dangling out of the window and I dropped safely to earth outside.

As we closed the window and snaked our way across the yard with heavy breaths and hearts racing, I wondered why Uncle Bernie had lied to me about the chest, and what exactly he was hiding.

I wasn't going to think about the things I was hiding, or how my own lies were piling up.

Chapter 14

Sleep was a defiant son of a gun. It didn't help that I was a lying, cheating, Jonah-kissing betrayer.

I tossed and turned for hours, eyelids like anvils, miserable, desperate for sleep. For a blissful moment I would slip into a deep well of rest, my mind numb and pliable, then my body would resist, jolting me awake.

When I finally did fall asleep, thank God I didn't dream about Jonah's kiss. Instead I dreamt about unlocking the chest, opening it, and finding Cordelia's rotting corpse inside. I really hoped there were no cadavers in the real-life trunk, though I'd be willing to rummage through a pile of bones if it meant finding out what secrets Cordelia hid. If only unlocking Uncle Bernie's secrets was as easy as dreaming.

I staggered from my bedroom in my PJs, scratching a bad case of bed head with one hand and clutching the key in the other. I found my father in his home office, head buried in the *Bloodson Bay Bulletin* where the front-page article addressed local politics—particularly Judge Ewan Valance's reelection campaign. The photo showed him in his signature ten-gallon Stetson, a jackass-eating-briars grin plastered on his flabby face, as usual, as he pressed the flesh. I stuck my tongue out at him.

Dad was so absorbed in whatever he was reading—presumably sports—that I sidled up to him, standing behind him without his knowing. When I spoke, he started in his spinning leather chair, spilling coffee on the already brown circle-stained stack of papers on his desk.

"A load of garbage if you ask me," Dad grumbled, folding the newspaper. "Politicians are nothing but corrupt liars," he added, before glancing up at me.

"What about you, Dad? You're the mayor."

Dad swiveled his chair around to face me. "Well, except for me. I'm clean as a whistle."

Sure he was.

"Can I show you something?" I asked, eager to change the subject.

"Of course. I need a break from this bird cage liner anyway."

"Have you ever seen this before?" I opened my palm in front of him, revealing the key.

He picked it up, examining the detail. "Where did you find this?"

I couldn't tell him I had snuck into Uncle Bernie's trailer and stolen it, so I blurted out the first thing that came to mind:

"I found it in the barn."

The barn? As soon as I said it I regretted my obvious lie.

112

"That's an odd place for someone to leave it."

"Maybe someone dropped it." *Lame.* "Do you know what it opens?"

"I sure do."

I perked up, excited to be one step closer to unlocking the chest...if only I could now *find* the chest.

"It opens the door to the Bloodson family mausoleum."

My heart deflated. It wasn't the key to the chest after all. But a family crypt sounded pretty incredible nonetheless.

"We have a mausoleum?"

"I could have sworn your mom and I took you and your brother there before to show you. You don't remember?"

"No, I don't think so. Where is it at?"

"In the Bloodson Bay Cemetery. It's a big red brick crypt with an iron gate around it. Supposedly all of our family members dating back to Reginald and Cordelia Bloodson are buried there. Somewhere along the line their remains were moved from our family plot to the town cemetery for legal reasons."

That explained why the family graveyard we'd stumbled upon was abandoned and overgrown. "Is there anything else there?"

He scratched his chin. "Hanging along the interior walls are metal plaques that tell the story of how Bloodson Bay was founded, which you might find interesting. You're like your mom and Uncle Bernie in that regard— all history buffs."

"I can't believe I don't remember it."

"You were pretty young when we took you, but anyway, this key unlocks the door to it. You should check it out sometime. But don't lose this key. We only have one original left ever since the copy went missing years ago. Imagine it turning up in Bloodson Manor ..."

A family vault sounded exactly like the kind of place that might have the answers I was looking for.

**

Come twilight, Bloodson Bay Cemetery was draped in stony silence. Not a breeze stirring or a wisp of grass waving. A choir of crickets, katydids, and tree frogs lifted their voices in a raucous lament for the dead...which, I feared, threatened to wake them. Tension between Chris and Tara was palpable, but I hoped they could push it aside for my brother's sake. For all our sakes, really. Jonah and I kept our distance too.

At the front gate that led into the cemetery was a blue-green oxidized plaque giving the history of the cemetery.

"It says here that the cemetery was founded after the Civil War in 1865, when the citizens demanded plots to bury their loved ones after the dead bodies started piling up."

"Ew, that's morbid," Tara replied.

"It's a cemetery, sis. The whole thing's morbid," Jonah retorted.

Tara looked worried as dusk thickened around us. "Do you really think there's something here that will help us figure out what caused the original grudge between the Valances and the Bloodsons?"

"I'm hoping so. First we need to find out more about Gertrude Bloodson, and if the feud had anything to do with her. There's a reason Gertrude and her husband were buried in the family plot, but why weren't any other Valances after her buried there? Something must have happened after she died that caused the rift."

We meandered through rows of crumbling gravestones, some representing several generations of families, others a solitary individual here and there. Family names dating all the way back to the 1860s dotted the grounds, and it was easy to tell their social status based on the size of the memorial. Adorned with cherubs with broken wings, or kneeling lambs with begrimed sandstone fleeces, the children's and infants' markers were especially heartbreaking. Some were victims of smallpox, scarlet fever, and influenza epidemics, and some had died at birth, or shortly thereafter. I hurried past these, as if I could feel tiny hands clutching at my ankles from beneath the sod.

The oldest section, dedicated to Bloodson Bay's fallen Confederate soldiers, contained neat rows of simple, round-topped marble headstones moldering in the shade of ancient live oaks. High atop his pedestal overgrown with English ivy, a stone soldier cradled his musket at parade rest, standing vigil in the center of the verdant space—

looking South, of course. Chris and Jonah, incurable smart-asses that they were, marched in lockstep past the memorial, discordantly warbling "Dixie."

Without the names in any order, it took forever before Tara found one she recognized. "I found all the Valances over here. Including Edgar and Gertrude's headstones."

"So they were removed from the family plot too. What's the point in digging up and reburying coffins?" Jonah asked.

"You can't just have bodies buried in people's backyards, Jonah," Tara said.

Further into the cemetery the Spanish moss hung from bare branches in feathery curtains. Smack-dab in the middle we found the huge monument dedicated to our ancestors. A small brick building with a rusting wrought iron gate surrounding it. A stone tablet etched with the words *Bloodson Family, Founders of Bloodson Bay* hung on the front wall beside a pair of wooden doors with two rings in the middle that served as door handles.

The gate swung open with a scream, and we walked the overgrown stone pathway to the entrance. The lock on the left door matched the lock on the chest, with the crown and dagger on each side of the keyhole. I shot the others a here-goes-nothing glance and inserted the key. The rusty tumblers groaned in protest, then the lock turned with a satisfying snick.

Grabbing both rings, the doors opened with a firm pull. A wave of musty air poured over us as we entered, my

116

pupils slowly adjusting to the gloom. I searched my backpack for the flashlight I made sure to bring—with brand-new batteries this time.

The inside of the mausoleum had clearly suffered neglect. I wasn't sure if the floor was packed earth or really dirty concrete. The building consisted of two rooms. The front room had a granite bench running alongside one wall, and in the back room on the other side of an arched brick doorway I saw floor-to-ceiling rows of square tiles the size of caskets. Little metal rectangles listed various generations of Bloodson family members.

On the bench was a vase holding crispy dried flowers. I wondered how long ago they had been placed here. It looked like at least before I was born, judging by the inch-thick film of dust covering it.

The brick wall above the bench was lined with huge metal plates. I passed the light over each of them, reading aloud the inscription of a story that continued from panel to panel:

In 1817, Reginald Bloodson and his closest companion, Doctor Edgar Valance, headed southbound from Ohio in search of a new beginning. After arriving at an unclaimed parcel of coastal North Carolina, they fell in love with the rich soil, and with the bay, whose natural defenses against storm surges earmarked it as an ideal port. Thus they claimed the tract as their own.

After building a house, Reginald farmed the land, finding it perfect for cotton and tobacco crops. While Edgar had set his sights on continuing southward to Savannah to advance his medical career, Reginald convinced him of the prosperity that would benefit them both if he stayed.

Soon word got out about this ideal farmland, and Reginald's sister, Gertrude, joined him. As people heard about the thriving crops, many came and settled in the area, helping to build the town.

Once the town was established, an immigrant woman named Cordelia arrived, and Reginald knew he had met his true love. To impress her, he built Bloodson Manor, a three-story house along the bay. In 1822 they wedded in the town church and began growing their family.

Doctor Edgar Valance went on to marry Gertrude and served as the town doctor. As Reginald was the wealthiest landowner and considered the town's founder, this inspired the townsfolk to name the town Bloodson Bay posthumously after his tragic death.

Chris had been quiet up until now. "It's interesting that no one even knows about that Dr. Edgar Valance guy being one of the people who helped establish the town. As a fellow founder, do you think that might have pissed him off that he got no credit—and that's what started the bad blood?"

"I know that would piss me off," Jonah agreed.

"Even if that's what started the friction between your families," Tara chimed in, "it has nothing to do with the missing body at Bloodson Manor. I thought that was the whole reason we were looking into this—to solve that murder. This whole thing is giving me a headache."

"We *are* trying to solve that murder," I explained. "But I'm pretty sure it's all connected to the house. Cordelia's death, Reginald's death, the Valance vendetta, the missing body—all of those events happened at the house. They're all linked. I just need to figure out *how*."

While Chris and Tara wandered into the second room of the vault, Jonah hung back as if waiting to talk privately with me. I already knew I did not want this conversation. Not now, maybe not ever.

"I hope I didn't make things weird between us," he began.

"Well, they weren't weird until now," I replied with a laugh. "Look, I'll always care about you, Jonah. We grew up together. But I like staying just friends. It's nothing against you. I just…it's just how I feel. I'm sorry."

Looking down at his feet, Jonah kicked a stone. "The friend zone. I get it. I just hoped that maybe eventually you could see me as more than that."

He looked up, meeting my stare just long enough to shoot a thrilling tingle through my body. Maybe I *did* like Jonah like that. Or maybe it was the dank chill of the vault sending shivers across my skin.

"Speaking of friends…where are Tara and Chris?"

"They must have gone deeper into the crypt."

Advancing into the pitch-black room, we walked in just in time for my beam to catch Chris in the corner as he leaned in to plant a kiss on Tara's cheek. A moment later her fist swung toward his face, hitting him square in the jaw.

"Oh my gosh, I'm so sorry! I didn't mean to punch you like that!" she exclaimed as Chris stepped back, rubbing his chin.

"That wasn't the response I was hoping for." Chris laughed, but it sounded awfully close to crying. "You could have just said you didn't like me."

"No, it's not that I don't like you. It was just…a reflex. I had no idea my hand would do that."

Chris had the good humor to laugh it off, since I could honestly say that he deserved a punch in the face once in a while. Though right now all I wanted to do was hug him.

While Chris nursed his mouth and ego, Jonah grabbed my arm. "Peace, I'm about to make your whole day."

I swept the beam over Jonah, standing in the far corner sporting an ear-to-ear grin, and jabbing his index finger toward the ground. I let the light travel down until it fell on the crown and dagger crest of…

Cordelia's trunk!

"Jonah, I could kiss you!" I blurted out. "Uh, I mean, way to go."

"Yeah, uh, thanks. I just kinda stumbled into it in the

dark."

Jonah knelt down and tugged at the lid. "Damn thing won't budge!" he grunted.

"Out of the way," I said, elbowing him aside in my excitement.

Kissing the skeleton key for good luck, I inserted it into the lock, twisted it, and heard a faint click.

"It worked!" Tara exclaimed.

All injured egos were forgotten as we celebrated the win. I opened the lid, anxious to see what secrets were buried inside. A myriad of objects, ancient and random, filled the box.

An old shaving kit wrapped in a leather pouch, sepia pictures, drawings, dried flowers, books...and as I rummaged down to where Cordelia had mentioned a false bottom, I lifted the corner of the base slightly, aiming the flashlight inside a fist-sized gap.

Then Chris said exactly what I was thinking: "What the heck is *that* for?"

Chapter 15

I trained the flashlight on the object Chris held in his hand. A brown prescription bottle.

"It says it's anti-hysteria water," Chris said.

Indeed it did. I squinted and read the fine print aloud:

Used to treat hysteria and related symptoms, including nervousness, temper, suicidal thoughts, debility, sleeplessness, irritated throat, stomach pains, rheumatism, laziness, infertility, and more!

"Now *that's* some cure-all," Jonah observed.

The antique bottle had Gertrude Valance's name scrawled across the label; there was a second medicinal bottle, too, identical except for it lacked her name. I spied something equally curious in the hiding place and pulled it out for a closer look. It was a long metal probe with a ball and joint at one end and a circular piece of metal attached to the other end where the handle was. It took a minute for me to realize what it was, then I dropped it in disgust.

"Gross! I can't believe there's a uterine elevator in here."

"A uterine elevator?" said Chris. "Sounds like something out of a horror movie."

"Pretty close. Back then they believed the uterus moved around in a woman's body, and a wandering womb could cause mental problems and fertility issues. So they would shove this contraption inside her to adjust the uterus. It was one of many horrifying Victorian remedies for"—then I air-quoted this—"'female hysteria.'"

Chris snorted. "What makes you such an expert?"

"I don't claim to be an expert, dumbass. It just happens that I wrote a term paper on the wackadoodle medical practices of the Victorian age—especially as they related to women's health—for my senior social studies class. Got an A, naturally."

"Naturally. *Geek.*"

"But what exactly is *female hysteria*?" Jonah asked.

"In the Victorian era that was the blanket diagnosis for people—though mostly women—suffering from anxiety or depression or panic attacks, or even epilepsy. If they didn't know what it was and you were acting strange, they called it *hysteria* and did all kinds of crazy stuff to"—another set of air quotes—"'cure' you."

"What other kinds of crazy stuff?" Grimacing, Jonah dangled the uterine elevator between his thumb and index finger as if he was afraid it might bite him. Or catch a disease from it.

"Hydrotherapy, where they sprayed you with cold water. Some doctors went to extremes like performing lobotomies. It was barbaric." I paused, grinning mischievously. "Then there was the steam-powered vibrator they called the 'Manipulator.'" That kinky reference got everyone's attention. "Never mind, y'all aren't old enough to know about that. I'm not even sure *I'm* old enough."

I had barely begun to scratch the surface of the horrors that the medical field called *cures*, when a loud slam plunged us into sudden darkness.

"Hey, what happened?" Tara screamed.

"Don't worry. The door just blew shut." Chris slowly felt his way to the entrance. When he rattled the door handle and I didn't hear it open, I knew something was wrong.

I joined Chris, and together we shoved our shoulders into the door. It cracked open a little, but something on the other side held it shut.

"Someone blocked us in here!" Tara moaned. She and Jonah had come up beside us. "We're all gonna die!"

"Jeez, Tara," I said, "take a chill pill already. Let's look at this logically. If some pranksters blocked the door, they're long gone by now. We can't get out by ourselves, but maybe the caretaker will hear us if we make enough noise."

"You think this dump's got a caretaker?" said Chris. "Dream on."

"It's worth a try." *If he hasn't gone home.* I kept that thought to myself.

For a good three minutes we screamed at the top of our lungs, and pounded on the door for good measure, until our voices were hoarse and our palms were raw. Only the night bugs and the frogs answered.

"Well, so much for that brilliant idea," said Jonah. "But my question is, who the hell locked us in here?"

"I have a feeling I know," Chris seethed. "Victor Valance has been gunning for us. I bet my life it's him who did this. He's clearly watching us."

"What makes you think that?" I wasn't trying to defend Vic, but we needed more than a hunch.

"He just *happened* to show up at the Slaughter Shed when we were there. And I wouldn't be shocked if he's the one who let the horses out. Hell, he probably took the chest and hid it here."

"But why would he want to hide the chest? What's the point?"

"Because he clearly knows something about the family history that he doesn't want made public."

Jonah seemed doubtful. "Like what? What would be bad enough that he would need to keep it hidden?"

"Don't you see? His ancestor Edgar Valance must have tortured his own wife Gertrude, who was a Bloodson, by the way. You think that anti-hysteria medicine with her name on it, and the uterine thingy used to treat hysteria, are in that chest together by coincidence? Cordelia hid it in that fake bottom for a reason! Edgar was the town doctor— and my bet is he was brutalizing his wife and Cordelia knew about it."

I ran with Chris's logic. "Right, and Cordelia might have even stood up to Dr. Valance to protect Gertrude from him…"

"And Cordelia might have been killed for it! Think about it—she survived four births up until now. Maybe she didn't die from childbirth. Maybe her own doctor killed her," Chris concluded.

"I can imagine Judge Valance would do anything to prevent the news of his murderous ancestor coming out during his reelection campaign."

Jonah scoffed. "You really think voters care what some obscure doc did more than a century ago? Get real."

"You're wrong, Jonah," I said. "Look at the Lizzie Borden case, which if you remember anything about from history class, it happened in the 1890s and they *still* do tours of the murder house. There's been a buttload of books and songs and films devoted to her case. People love a good murder mystery…especially an unsolved one in a small town. Murder never gets old, and being related to the town's most notorious killer never goes away. We would know—we changed our last name because of it."

A puzzle piece fell into place in my head.

"Chris, you said the Valance brothers dared you to go inside the Slaughter Shed last year, which is when you saw the dead body, right?"

He nodded.

"So they were there last year, then again we found

126

them there this year. Think about it—why are they there every year? I think Chris is right. The Valance family is connected to everything. They probably saw the body and might have had something to do with its disappearance."

I admit it was a very weak thread, frayed and thin, but it was the only lead we had to finding out who had been hanging in Bloodson Manor, and why.

"How do you even know they went into the house after Chris came running out?" Jonah asked.

"Oh come on. If some kid comes running out of a haunted house screaming about a dead body, wouldn't you want to see it for yourself?"

"Touché," Jonah agreed.

"Did they ever say anything about it afterward?" I asked Chris.

"No, that's the weird part. The next day I asked them about it, and they acted like nothing had happened. Like I was crazy and seeing things. That's what convinced me that maybe I *was* seeing things. Maybe it wasn't real. But that rope we found confirmed that it was real. So they must have done something with the body, right?"

There was only one way to find out. "We need to ask them about it."

"Ha! Good luck getting anything but lies from them."

"Even if their family is behind all of this, it's not going to get us out of this crypt," Jonah griped.

"Like I said, we're all gonna die!"

Tara had been silent all through our debate, until now.

I wanted to smack some sense into her, but with no windows, no way out, and nobody to come to our rescue, maybe the doom-and-gloom diva was right.

"Yeah, it sure looks like we're up a creek without a paddle. Unless…" I pointed to the pager clipped to Jonah's hip. "Are you able to send messages with that?"

"No, only receive them."

"What's the friggin' point of a beeper?" Chris cut in. "Are you a drug dealer now? Because I know you're not a doctor."

"Pagers are cool," Jonah protested.

"Yeah, like two years ago," Chris muttered.

Tara shuffled her way to the bench and lay down on the slab. "I'm not feeling so good." She didn't sound so good either, her voice barely above a whisper. "Did I mention I'm claustrophobic?" She grinned weakly. I shone the beam on her face; it was as white as a stick of chalk.

"That would have been helpful information *before* we got locked in," Chris joked, but we were all too anxious to laugh. "Hey, I promise you we'll get out. Just close your eyes and focus on breathing."

I could hear Tara's panic surge as her breaths became rapid and frantic.

"It's really warm in here," she continued, words tumbling together. "I'm…I'm…" Her breaths seized up as she tried to stand, wobbling on her feet, then tipping back onto the bench.

Chris caught her just before her body slumped into a

heap.

"Guys, I think Tara passed out!" Chris was caught in a frenzy, and I felt it coming for me next. "I'm going to kill Victor Valance as soon as we get out of here," he vowed. "I just know he's behind all of this!"

The Diary of Cordelia Bloodson

June 16, 1836

Today Doctor Valance performed another uterine elevator treatment on Gertrude. My heart aches for my dear sister and her broken body. I confronted Edgar about the anti-hysteria medicine I had found in Gertrude's clutch, and he insists it will help her. Yet I suggested to her that dedicating time for her artwork might be a better salve than the medical treatments.

Last night, waking me from my light slumber, an apparition approached me. It picked up the flowers at my bedside and carried them around the bedroom. At first I thought perhaps it was the wind, yet that theory was disproved as the bouquet stood collected in a neat upright bunch the entire flight across the room. It was both terrifying and exhilarating. I hope to never meet that specter again.

I have become increasingly exhausted, as the baby is due

any day. Reginald has cloaked himself in impenetrable irritability. I suspect it has something to do with the letter that slipped out of my diary onto the floor. I am now certain Reginald read Edgar's proposal to me.

I would never dare tell Reginald that I myself had been irresistibly drawn to the good doctor, and that his words, from the depths of his heart, had quickly wooed me. But I had been brought up to look upon marriage as a step to be taken not lightly, nor hurriedly, especially as my heart leaned toward another beau, my dear Reginald. If only he understood I had chosen him from the very moment we met, and I would forever choose him. Even still, despite his moods.

The guilt of denying Edgar still weighs heavy, not only because of the rejection he suffered at my hand, but also for crushing his dreams by imploring him to stay in this dull, provincial town, rather than journeying to Savannah, and perfecting his clinical expertise in that charming cosmopolitan city. All of this sacrifice for me, a girl who ended up wedding another man. I had felt such joy when he married Gertrude, but that joy has burned to ash as I see their strife mount with each miscarriage.

I know not how to help any of them, least of all myself.

Chapter 16

Tara was passed out on the bench while Chris tried to nudge her awake. Jonah paced from one end of the mausoleum to the other, throwing out every swear word he could think of…and he had quite a creative selection of them.

According to my Indiglo watch, we had been stuck in here for hours. And I was starting to freak out just a little.

After testing the blockade's limits, I had been able to push the doors open a sliver, allowing a small slice of lingering daylight through. Which meant something directly outside of them was holding them shut, and it might be possible to break through.

Despite Chris and Jonah's joint effort to ram the doors, they kept bouncing back and closing. Something had to be wrapped around the rings tying them together, since we would have seen any other large obstruction through the opening. Pressing my face up against it, I caught a glimpse of some kind of fabric around where the rings were.

Fabric was cuttable.

"Hey, I think I could saw through whatever is holding the doors shut. Did anyone happen to bring a pocketknife with them?" One could only hope.

"No, it never occurred to me that someone would try to lock us in a crypt," Jonah replied sarcastically.

Rooting through the chest, I found all kinds of random items, but nothing with a blade. Except hadn't I seen a shaving kit in here—presumably with a shaving knife? As I dug deeper, I found the leather kit at the bottom. I opened the folding razor and ran my fingertip along the straight-edged blade. Yep, this could definitely kill a man, or saw through something.

"This might work!" I exclaimed and ran to the doors.

While the boys pushed against them to give me enough of a gap to slide the blade through, I sawed away. It wasn't fabric like I had expected, though. It was some kind of thick leather strap.

Eventually I cut through it and the doors swung open. Chris carried Tara outside to the fresh air, whispering over her. It would have been sweet if it wasn't so scary. When she came to in his arms, she wrapped herself around him, sobbing her thanks. I had to wipe away a tear or two at the sappiness of it.

I grabbed the cut leather straps on our way out. Evidence that would hopefully lead me to who did it so I could beat the crap out of them. It was a belt, wrapped and buckled around the rings. The tacky oversized belt buckle was still attached, embossed with the vainglorious V.

It was a total giveaway.

Stupid, stupid boy.

"I know who locked us in." It wouldn't be a surprise to anyone when I confirmed it. We had already guessed as much.

"Who?"

I held up the belt buckle up for inspection.

"It was that assface Victor and his assface brother Leonard!" Jonah yelled.

"I knew it! Like I said," Chris added, "they probably let the horses out, hoping we'd lose half our herd or die trying to save them. They were already trespassing on our property. It wouldn't take more than a short detour to open the gate on the way to the Slaughter Shed."

"That's twice that they almost got us killed," Jonah raged.

I waved this conversation to an end. "No, there is no way Leo would risk our horses' lives...or ours."

They all glared at me. Coming to Leo's defense was the worst possible thing I could say.

"How do *you* know?" Jonah eyed me skeptically.

"I just know. Leo would never try to hurt us."

"The broken nose he gave me last year says otherwise."

Jonah and Leo had been constant enemies since middle school. Before now I had never understood why, though I was beginning to make sense of their rivalry.

"Leo has changed," I insisted. "He's not like that anymore. Besides, I know that fight last year wasn't one-sided. You both push each other's buttons."

"I bet I know what—or *who*—they were fighting over..." Chris looked at me.

I looked at Jonah.

And Jonah looked at his feet. "Shut up!"

"Guys, stop it! We need to tell the cops what happened tonight," Tara interrupted sternly. "We could have died in there if we hadn't gotten out. No one would have found us for days. We could have starved or gotten dehydrated!"

"What do you think the cops will say?" Jonah replied. "You know the po-po are on Judge Valance's payroll. He controls this town. No one will believe us."

"And even if they do," Chris put in, "Victor will just say it was a harmless prank and he was going to let us out. The cops will do nothing and we'll end up looking stupid."

"You're right," I agreed.

"So we're just going to let them get away with it?" Tara said. "You've got to be kidding me!"

I shook my head. "No, I have a much better idea for how to deal with them."

Chapter 17

By the time we hauled the chest to my red Subaru station wagon parked along the curb, the sky was darker than the inside of a closed crypt. I could say that now with the conviction of one who had been locked in a crypt.

With all four of us carrying a side, we were able to lift it most of the way, dragging it a couple times across the grass when Tara exhausted herself. I held my breath as I closed the hatchback, only breathing easy when the door closed and the huge trunk fit.

Sneaking it past my parents, who were watching *Friends* in the living room, and up the stairs was another feat altogether. Especially with weak-armed Tara, who hadn't spent her childhood mucking stalls and building farmgirl muscles like I had.

Eventually we dropped it with a *thunk* on my bedroom floor and crowded around it. Tara plopped face-first on my furry leopard-print bedspread while Chris dropped into my beanbag chair. Behind him hung a Backstreet Boys poster that I was suddenly embarrassed to own, let alone put on display.

I wiped sweat off my brow and searched my pocket for

the key.

"Are you okay?" Chris asked, and I looked up to find him talking to Tara, who looked awfully pale.

"I'm just shaken up, I think. And thirsty."

Chris moved from the chair to the bed and wrapped his arm around her. She rested her head on his shoulder. It was so perfectly, enviably sweet. If only my own love life was that simple.

"Get a room, guys." Jonah was joking, but jealousy lurked beneath the jab. I knew he wanted that same closeness for us, but I always held it out of reach.

"I'll get you something to drink," Chris offered, touching Tara's cheek lightly.

"I'll come with you."

Chris led Tara by the hand out of my bedroom, leaving Jonah and me alone. I had been trying to avoid this scenario, especially after the kiss.

The kiss I loathed and yet couldn't forget.

I pulled the key out of my jeans and knelt down in front of the trunk. My hand trembled as I felt the cold hardness in my palm. After everything that had happened the past couple days—the weird goings-on at Bloodson Manor, the escaped horses that nearly stampeded off the cliff, nearly getting caught sneaking into Uncle Bernie's house, the kiss that should never have happened, getting locked in a crypt—my nerves were shot. I was barely holding it together.

Jonah rested his hand on mine, warming it, calming it.

I dared not risk looking at him. I couldn't be liable for anything I did if our eyes met.

"You're okay. I'm always here for you, even if I'm stuck in the friend zone," he said, and the words actually soothed me. I knew he meant them.

"Thanks, Jonah."

I didn't have anything else to say. No promise to offer. I knew he wanted more from me, and part of me wanted to give it freely. I depended on him. He'd been a constant in my life I could always rely on, but I was outgrowing him. We were both just starting our lives, and after this summer we would inevitably grow apart. Although I hadn't enrolled in college, who knew where I would land? Probably not Bloodson Bay. Seemed like the only way a Bloodson—and I was one to the bone, no matter what my driver's license said—ever got out of this crummy town was by dying an ignoble death. I wasn't about to stick around this burg and let that happen to me.

So any kind of relationship was doomed. What else could I do but protect both our hearts?

Holding my hand steady, he guided it toward the lock, and together we inserted the key and turned it. After the click I waited for Jonah to let go, but he didn't. He simply looked at me with tears in his eyes, a question clearly burning his tongue.

"I'll never have a chance, will I?" he finally asked.

Why did he have to ask? Why did he want me to break his heart all over again?

"Please don't..." My voice trailed away, along with his fingers as he released me.

Chris and Tara's voices traveled up the stairwell. Jonah took a hasty step away from me as they entered my bedroom laughing. I opened up the chest, revealing much more contents than I had been able to see in the dark mausoleum.

I began leafing through some of the papers. A newspaper article dated back to 1867. June 27, to be exact. The headline read:

MAN FALLS FROM CLIFF UNDER MYSTERIOUS CIRCUMSTANCES

The article went on to describe how thirty-one-year-old Sigmund Bloodson fell to his death from Bloodson Manor cliff, exactly thirty years after the date of his father's death.

"Sigmund Bloodson," I murmured aloud. "That must have been Reginald's fifth son."

I continued reading about how the case had stumped the authorities. A witness, later identified as Sigmund's wife, claimed she heard Sigmund arguing with someone shortly before his death. His Aunt Gertrude Valance had corroborated the testimony, claiming he had been fighting with a visitor, and had gone for a walk along the cliff to clear his mind. Slipping on a patch of unstable soil, he fell from the bluff in the same way of his father before him.

The June 27 curse was becoming more real with each life that Bloodson Manor stole.

Another newspaper clipping advertised the sale of the Bloodson estate, lock, stock, and barrel. I imagined that Sigmund's death prompted his grieving family to want to sell the house and its cursed cliff and get as far away from it as possible. Apparently it never sold, even though the family moved out. Who would want a house cursed with deadly, unexplained accidents?

I was still curious why Cordelia had hidden the anti-hysteria bottles in a secret compartment. They were common medicines back then, so why all the cloak-and-dagger? I pulled out the first bottle, rereading the label: *Anti-Hysteria Water*

This one didn't have a name scribbled on it, as I noted earlier. I peeked inside the bottle, where a crusty residue ringed the inside. I set the bottle aside, wondering what else we'd find.

Searching deeper in the chest, I found the other anti-hysteria bottle with Gertrude's name on it, and read the label of a third bottle that was a bit larger: *Cocaine Tablets*

Across the top of that label Reginald Bloodson's name had been written.

Jonah's eyes almost popped out of their sockets. "Cocaine? They prescribed that stuff back then?"

"Yeah, they used it to treat all kinds of things," I explained.

The typed label listed the medicinal's common uses:

Used to treat toothaches, depression, sinusitis, lethargy, alcoholism, and impotence! The miracle cure!

Cordelia had mentioned in her diary that Reginald had been acting sullen and depressed. Constantly irritable and angry, hallucinating and lashing out at people who weren't there.

Based on the prescriptions alone, it sounded like the whole Bloodson family was either depressed or insane. Gertrude was diagnosed with hysteria, Cordelia was paranoid about dying, and Reginald was being treated for moodiness. Each of them had been touched by the curse in a different way: Gertrude lost her baby, Cordelia died during childbirth, and Reginald killed his children, then himself; Sigmund simply fell—which I had my doubts about. The deeper I dug, the more I discovered, the more I feared I was slipping down the same deadly path.

An obsession with solving the mystery possessed me, body and soul.

Why couldn't I let it go?

Had the curse taken hold of me too?

The only one who seemed untouched by it all was Dr. Edgar Valance. Which seemed awfully suspicious to me.

I went to my bookshelf to my collection of *Encyclopedia Britannicas* that I had begged Dad to buy me for Christmas a couple years ago. Pulling out the *C* volume, I paged through it until I found what I was looking for. I began reading aloud:

"Common side effects of cocaine overdosing include euphoria, panic, irritability, and seizures. It can also cause one to experience extreme anxiety and depression. Long-term use may lead to psychosis, hallucinations, and paranoia. This mood instability can result in irritability and aggressive behavior as well as depression."

Tara's eyes sparked with understanding. She knew where I was headed with this. "You think Dr. Valance was overdosing Reginald with the intention of killing him. Or at least making him lose his mind."

"It's the perfect murder. Make someone do the dirty work for you. If Reginald had been taking cocaine for depression, Dr. Valance could have prescribed him too much, causing him to overdose and kill his family."

Another puzzle piece clicked into place.

"What about the dead body Chris saw last year hanging in Bloodson Manor? Do you still think that's somehow connected?"

That part I still hadn't figured out yet. I could be on a wild goose chase, for all I knew.

Tara held up the two anti-hysteria bottles and waved me over. "Look here. If you compare these two bottles, this one that wasn't prescribed for Gertrude has some kind of crust inside it. Do you think he slipped something in one of them?"

"Maybe. But I can't think of any reason for Dr. Valance to want his wife dead."

"Me neither," Chris chimed in. "And remember, Gertrude didn't die under suspicious circumstances. She actually outlived them all. So how do you explain that?"

I couldn't. Unless the doctor had tried to poison his wife but it didn't work. I wondered if Cordelia's diary might shed some light on any juicy stuff about Edgar and Gertrude's marriage.

I slid the diary out from its hiding place under my mattress and flipped through the entries. A letter fell out from an entry dated June 20, 1836. I unfolded it and read the first sentence under my breath:

It is time for me to expose my sins.

"Whoa, it's a letter from Dr. Valance to Cordelia."

"What does it say?" Chris asked.

"It sounds like some sort of confession…"

Another puzzle piece. *Click.*

But before I started reading it aloud, the stomp of boots rose from the stairwell.

"Peace? Chris?" It was Uncle Bernie. And he sounded pissed.

"We've got to hide the trunk!" I whispered. I pointed to my closet. "In there!"

Slamming the lid shut, we shoved the chest across the floor—leaving huge scratches on the hardwood that I would have to hide from my parents later—toward the closet. I yanked the folding door shut just as Uncle Bernie appeared in the doorway.

"What's up, Uncle Santa?"

Uncle Bernie wasn't buying Jonah's innocent act.

"Shut up, squirt. I'm not your uncle." He pivoted his attention to me. "Peace, I know you were snooping in my trailer. I know what you took. Give it back. Now." He held out his calloused palm.

I decided to play dumb. I refused to give up the key.

"What *are* you talking about?" I asked coyly, adopting a honeyed accent.

"I had a key, and it's gone. And I know you took it."

"Uncle Bernie, I have no idea what you're talking about. A key to *what*?" Academy Award, here I come!

Uncle Bernie almost looked convinced. "A key to…" He paused and thought for a moment. "There's no point lying to me. Your mother already told me you had it."

Busted.

"Oh, *that* key. Um, yeah, we found it in the barn."

"In the barn? That makes no sense…unless…" I'd never seen blood drain from a face until now. Uncle Bernie's voice dropped to a distracted whisper, along with his worried gaze. "Your mom told me the horses got out a couple nights ago, didn't she? And then the key in the barn…no, he wouldn't do that to make a point," he muttered, "would he?"

"Would who do what?" Chris asked.

144

Uncle Bernie suddenly glanced back at us, as if he'd been in another world and discovered ours for the first time. He looked shocked to see us. And scared.

"Nothing. No one. Don't worry about it. Just give me the key."

I pulled it out of my pocket and handed it to him.

He shuffled out, then popped his head back through the doorway. "Do not, under any circumstances, return to that house. You hear me?"

When we didn't answer right away, he repeated, "Do. You. Hear. Me?"

"We won't go back to the house," I spoke up for the group. "Promise."

"Sure you won't."

He clomped down the stairs, and we heard the front door slam.

"What was that about?" Chris said.

"I don't know," I admitted, "but I think Uncle Bernie's in some deep doo-doo."

The Diary of Cordelia Bloodson

June 20, 1836

I found a letter slipped under my bedroom door this afternoon. It is from the good doctor, and I pray Reginald and Gertrude never read this, lest this confession destroy us all:

My darkest secret, Cordelia:

It is time for me to expose my sins.

I am to leave shortly for Savannah, having accepted a medical apprenticeship involving experimentation with new fertility treatments that promise hope in Gertrude one day birthing me a child. Thus, I feel I must write this confession before I go. Let us leave no secrets between us.

You once told me you loved me, and I believed you. But when you chose Reginald over me, my life became untold hours of ceaseless misery, for I felt a love that crowded out all desire for anything else but you. That night I retired early and wept so bitterly at hearing of your love for another man that I well-nigh made myself ill. I could even forgive Reginald for keeping me in this dismal town, if I only had your heart instead.

After years of struggling to accept you belonged to another, I swallowed my pride and vowed, "I will crush the feelings I have for you and simply look upon you as one dead, and let your sweet memory be as a candle to light my darkest hours."

Yet the dark hours are so long I can hardly bear their torment. Love and happiness are the deepest needs of the human spirit; they go hand in hand, heart in heart. And as I love you utterly, so have you now become the whole world of my spirit. Cordelia, my darling, you are so fine, so indescribably lovely that to be near you, to gaze upon your face, to hear your mellifluous voice, is now the only happiness, the only life, I want. And yet I shall never possess it.

I am ashamed to confess that my best friend has become my bitter rival. And now your fifth child leaves my life feeling even emptier. The choice has become clear as my resentment toward you and Reginald grows feral, unpredictable, dangerous. Even Gertrude perceives my heart's absence. And so I must go, leaving behind the home I built here with my own two hands. Far from you, from the love that will not die. Perhaps distance will at long last free me from this eternal hell.

You may have loved me once, but I have loved you forever. Perhaps in the death of our love may we both find rebirth.

Yours eternally,

Edgar

Chapter 18

Sending Chris and Jonah on a reconnaissance mission seemed like the best way to keep them busy and out of juvie for the time being. Ever since getting locked in the mortuary, all they talked about was getting payback. So I decided to put that energy to good use. Their job: keep an eye on Victor. And for the love of God, don't pick a fight.

As long as they were following Victor, they were staying out of my hair. As for Tara and me, we had other details to attend to.

Debbie's Diner was open 24/7 and the most popular—and only—teenage hangout in Bloodson Bay after all the nine-to-five businesses closed for the day. Debbie offered greasy food cheap, which was everything starving teenagers could ask for.

Walking along the sidewalk, we followed the shiny chrome siding trimmed with red neon toward the entrance. The little bell jingled when I pulled open the fingerprint-smudged front door, and we headed to our favorite red vinyl booth.

"Our usual!" we called out.

"Comin' right up!" Debbie hollered back.

While we waited, Tara pulled her Tamagotchi from her purse and started feeding her pet digital creature inside its little pink egg-shaped computer. As an animal lover, it was a fad I held in contempt.

"I suppose you'd never consider getting a *real* pet," I said, frowning. "The shelters are full of cats and dogs needing forever homes, and here you are playing nursemaid to a freaking imaginary alien."

Tara, making cooing sounds to her charge, didn't even look up. "Who has the time for all that walking, grooming, and cleaning up poop?"

"I hope to God you'll change your mind someday. Now put that stupid thing away and let's talk!"

"Okay, okay! But if my alien baby dies from neglect, it's on you" She shoved the game back in her purse. "Whaddaya want to talk about?"

"The mystery. Duh!"

"Right. Actually, I've been thinking about that. I still can't believe that Dr. Valance had been in love with Cordelia, his own sister-in-law."

"It makes sense," I replied. "Love makes people do crazy things."

"Murdering your best friend to get his girl is pretty mental, though."

"Jealousy murder isn't that uncommon. Shakespeare built a whole brand on it."

Debbie placed our drinks and food—loaded cheese fries for me, double cheeseburger and onion rings for

Tara—on the table. She crossed her arms across her pillowy bosom and slowly shook her head.

"Look at you two sticks! If I ate like y'all do," she said, eyeballing us like livestock too puny to take to market, "I'd be as curvy as Roseanne Barr."

Which she was, but I wasn't about to say so. Debbie wasn't through making us feel guilty.

"*Humph.* Y'all just wait till y'all hit forty. It's all downhill from there." She shoved the ticket under the napkin holder. "Well, I've got the defibrillator warming up for you gals by the cash register." She lumbered off, cackling to herself.

While we chowed down on our respective heart-attacks-on-a-plate, I did a mental review of the mystery up to this point.

After reading Edgar's letter to Cordelia, I thought we had it all figured out. Well, at least I could sense we were close. We concluded that the seed of revenge was first planted when Reginald stole Edgar's credit as the town founder, getting rich off the land while Edgar's dream dwindled away. Because of Reginald, the doctor had passed up the opportunity to gain widespread respect working at a medical training apprenticeship in Savannah. In exchange he settled for being an undistinguished family doctor in a no-name town.

The salt in Edgar's wound was when Reginald stole Cordelia's heart, giving him his sister Gertrude as a consolation prize. It might not have been so bad if

Gertrude had been fertile like Cordelia, but with every baby Cordelia bore, Gertrude miscarried one after another. Every birth and every loss was another stab to Edgar's ego. And we all knew how fragile a male ego can be.

So Edgar attempted to poison Gertrude. Only, he hadn't expected her body to resist the poison. He even planned to leave Cordelia and Bloodson Bay behind, but he couldn't follow through in the end. What last resort was left? To kill Cordelia during childbirth and raise her baby as his own. The only problem were the other four kids and Reginald, who served as roadblocks to Edgar's villainous plan.

The best way to take them out was the slow and steady act of poisoning Reginald. While it would take a year to finally break him, all Edgar had to do was overprescribe Reginald cocaine until he went mad and killed everyone for him.

Stolen credit. Lost dreams. Unrequited love. Loss after loss. There were plenty of motives to drive Edgar to murder. And the body count was high enough, and Judge Valance's reputation precious enough, that he, like his prideful heinous ancestor, would kill to keep it secret.

Even with all of the puzzle pieces put together, I still felt like one was missing. The biggest piece.

When I thought back to the night in Bloodson Manor, my memory fell into a black hole. Some details stood out, like the rope and bloodstain and diary of course, but other details barely skimmed the surface. As if I had seen plenty of clues in the house that I couldn't quite put together.

"We have to go back," I blurted out.

"Go back where?" Tara asked, leaning toward me. Her strawberries and champagne perfume wafted toward me.

"To Bloodson Manor. There's something there we missed. I just feel it."

Tara just about choked on her last chug of Surge. "Oh, please! I don't know what you're trying to prove, Peace. We're not detectives or private investigators or the least bit qualified to do…whatever it is you're doing."

"Someone died last year, Tara. They deserve closure. I thought we were all on the same page about that."

"Exactly, Peace—someone is *dead*. Someone might have been *murdered*. We're kids! This is way bigger than us!"

"Instead you suggest we go to the same cops that might be the ones covering it up."

Tara looked away, clearly frustrated with me. "We don't even know if there ever was a body. We've got Chris's vague account, a piece of frayed rope, and a bloodstain on the floor. That doesn't exactly spell out murder. And if it does, we shouldn't be going toe-to-toe with a killer!"

The background chatter stopped, and a handful of diners swiveled their heads our way.

"I'm not going back, no way no how."

As Tara put that punctuation mark on the conversation, I realized she was right. They were just kids. I, however, was not.

Like my dad always said, if I wanted something done right, I would have to do it myself.

Chapter 19

"How about a movie night? I think we all could use a break from this whole creepy mystery."

I normally never thought my brother was right about anything, but this time I had to agree with Chris. We all needed a break.

"Alright, everyone to the station wagon!" I announced. "We're going to Blockbuster!"

As we turned into the Blockbuster parking lot, Jonah shouted "Padiddle!" and socked Chris in the shoulder as a Mustang with one headlight out cruised by us. The stupid game had been going on between Jonah and Chris ever since we left the house.

"That gives me two Padiddles," Jonah boasted. "If I get one more, I get to make a wish."

"I'm making a wish right now," I said. "That the Beavis and Butthead in my backseat would grow up."

"True that!" echoed Tara from the passenger seat.

"Uh," said Chris. "Which one am I—Beavis or Butthead?"

I frowned at him in the rearview. "Do you *really* want to know?"

"Right. I guess not."

I parked the car and we all piled out, discussing what movie genre we were all in the mood for. We were stuck between Comedy and Mystery. All the new releases had already been rented, so we ended up deciding on *Clueless* for us girls and *The Usual Suspects* for the guys. As I stood in the checkout line, I was surprised to see Leo Valance behind the counter. I knew he worked here, but I thought this was one of his nights off. Not that I'd paid *that* much attention to his schedule...

Unfortunately, Chris and Jonah had spotted him too and had revenge written all over their scowls. I stepped in front of them before they could head up to the counter.

"What's the big idea, Peace?" said Chris. "That creep, or his lowlife brother, probably caused the stampede. And trapped us in the crypt to boot."

"Yeah, we're gonna have it out with that creep," Jonah added.

"Whoa, little dogies, this ain't the O.K. Corral," I said. "I'll 'have it out' with him. You guys go on ahead to the car while I check out."

They obliged reluctantly, and I stepped up to the register and handed Leo my tapes.

"Well, fancy meeting you here," I said. "Thought you were off tonight, Leo."

"Hi, Peace. Filling in for a guy. I was hoping I'd run into you." Leo's nasally voice only became more prominent...and adorable. He seemed nervous.

"Yeah, me too. We need to talk about your brother."

Leo flexed his jaw muscles. I found that sexy as hell. "What about Vic?"

"He locked us in the crypt at the cemetery."

"I see. First of all, why were you in a crypt?"

"That's beside the point, Leo. But I know it was him because I found his belt holding the crypt door shut."

Earlier I had forgotten to take it out of my back pocket, so I showed him the incriminating belt buckle as proof. Grinning, Leo lifted up his blue polo shirt with yellow trim. My eyes feasted on his six-pack abs, then my attention was drawn to something else: a large bulge near the crotch of his skintight khakis. He either had something big in his pocket or else he was real glad to see me...

"Earth to Peace!"

"Huh? What?"

He pointed. "See the belt buckle?"

"Belt buckle? Oh, yeah." I shifted my gaze. There it was, the same exact tacky buckle as his brother's, with the same big V.

"Every Valance has that belt buckle. It's part of our brand, you might say. When did this happen?"

"Two nights ago."

Leo seemed visibly unnerved. "Then there's no way Vic did it, because he was traveling with my dad all day and they were out of town that night."

"Who else has this belt that would have locked us in? I need to know. We could have died in there, Leo."

"My brother can be a hothead, but he'd never cross that line. He's not a killer, Peace. I'm pretty sure all of the Valance cousins have that same belt too, but I can't think of any that would have a reason to do that."

I had my doubts that Leo knew his brother's true nature, but maybe he was right. Maybe Vic wasn't behind it, especially if he was in fact traveling. But if it wasn't Vic, who else could it be?

Leo shifted back to the register, scanning the videos and throwing a box of Reese's Pieces on the counter and ringing it up.

"What are you doing?" I asked.

"My treat," he said.

"How did you know those were my favorite candy?"

"I pay attention," he said, flashing a crooked grin.

I was flattered. I had gotten a box of Reese's Pieces a couple of times and the gorgeous lug actually remembered.

"I don't know how to thank you," I same lamely.

He gestured at the theater ticket-shaped blue and yellow sign on the counter. "You can thank me by being sure to do that."

Be Kind Rewind. "Funny," I said. It almost was. Boy, I had it bad for him!

He finished ringing me up and handed me my movies and candy. "You never did give me an answer about letting me take you out to dinner. Have you thought about it?"

Of course I had thought about it. Since he asked me on the date almost a month ago, I lived in constant guilt of keeping my feelings for him a secret from my family and friends. But I couldn't tell him any of this, because Leo didn't care what his family thought. He hated his dad. But I loved my family and spent my whole life wanting to please them. I couldn't become the family's black sheep over my crush on bad-boy Leonard Valance.

Instead of saying any of this, I kept it simple. And vague. Because I didn't want to lose Leo as much as I didn't want to lose my family...and I didn't want to hurt poor Jonah either. "It's just a really complicated situation, Leo. You know our families hate each other. How can I date a guy my parents...uh, don't exactly approve of?"

"Then don't consider it a date. Just dinner. Between friends."

"You know dinner is a date..."

"Not between two friends."

"Are you friend zoning me?" I grinned, lifting my eyebrow playfully. Ugh, and there I go flirting with him. I was terrible at this!

"If it means I can take you out to dinner, then yes."

"Leo..."

"Please, Peace. Tell me you don't like me back. If you can honestly tell me you have no feelings for me, then I'll back off and walk away. But if there's any chance you like me as much as I like you...just give me a chance to prove it won't end up as bad as you think it will."

"I'll think about it..." I conceded, totally smiling.

By now a line was forming behind me. I was already

pushing the door open to leave when a thought came to mind.

"Leo?" I called behind me.

He stopped mid-scan for the next customer to give me his attention.

"Let's do that dinner after all. How about tomorrow?"

Leo whooped so loudly I felt my cheeks burn red. I hoped he was still glad he asked once he found out what I had planned.

Chapter 20

After a late night of popcorn and candy and *As if*s and Keyser Söze, I convinced Tara, Chris, and Jonah that one more visit to Bloodson Manor wouldn't kill them. At least I hoped not.

My mind buzzed with thoughts that kept me awake all night. Thoughts about Jonah and Leo and this weird love triangle I was stuck in. But that was not the reason I couldn't sleep.

The Slaughter Shed had haunted me in my dreams, and I felt its dark presence even now in broad daylight as we broke through the woods into the clearing that overlooked the bay. The fog draped its milky veil across a calm quicksilver-gray ocean, its surface wrinkled only by a light breeze.

The four of us headed toward the front porch, Jonah and I leading with Chris and Tara a few steps behind. I paused to examine some letters carved into one of the posts as the group passed ahead of me. A memory was pried loose by the sight:

L <3 P

"What are you looking at?" Jonah asked.

"Nothing." I shifted to block it with my body.

I couldn't let anyone else see this. Especially not Jonah. Tara was reaching for the doorknob when Chris jumped in front of her, grabbing for it.

"Here, let me get that for you."

Tara backed away, exchanging a confused look with me. "Um, okay. Thanks?"

We all filed into the entry. Dust motes zoomed across the air, riding the sunbeams. Tara gasped and pointed to the large beams crossing the ceiling and scrollwork along the banisters.

"Look at the detail! In the daytime it's beautiful...if it wasn't so cursed."

Heading into the den, Tara began pulling a covering off of a desk. Rushing over to help her, Chris nudged her aside.

"I can do it for you."

Tara balled her fists on her skinny hips. "As if! I'm perfectly capable of doing it myself, Chris. What the heck is up with you?"

Chris shrunk back. "I'm sorry. I just want to be chivalrous."

Oh, now I understood. Tara searched my face for some kind of explanation, and I remembered the conversation I had with my brother about what girls want in a guy. I realized what he was doing. I pulled her aside while Chris struggled with the sheet snagging on something.

"This may have been my fault," I explained. "I told Chris he needed to be more...in control."

"In control? Of what?" Tara looked even more baffled.

"You know, being manly and taking care of you. You know he likes you, right?"

"I had thought it was pretty obvious. But lately he's acting so...weird."

"Look, guys are simpleminded creatures. When a guy likes a girl, he does one of two things: teases her relentlessly and makes her cry, or tries to take care of her and makes her helpless. Either way, he's just trying to give you his attention."

"But it's so annoying!" Tara whined.

"My suggestion is to lean into it and let him wait on you hand and foot. It makes him feel needed by you, and you get his undivided attention. It's a win-win!"

"I don't know...it feels demeaning."

"Enjoy it while you can, kid, because this attentiveness has a very short lifespan."

While the group decided to look through the furniture, opening drawers and lifting lids in search of clues, I headed out the back porch into a small overgrown garden. The scent was inviting, and I knelt down, digging my fingers into the breast of the black earth.

From this angle the house looked completely different, and I tried to envision which windows were for each room. At the very top I saw the tiny attic window and wondered if it was in this very spot where whoever had taken the chest had stood and watched us.

My gaze roamed back down the three floors, stopping on what appeared to be a cellar window. I headed over. The glass was caked with grime as I cupped my eyes trying to peer inside. I didn't remember seeing any basement steps in the house, but I imagined they couldn't be that hard to find.

I headed inside, roaming the perimeter of the first floor searching for the basement stairs. Every door led to another explored room, but no steps down.

There had to be some kind of hidden staircase…and I was determined to find out what was tucked away down there.

"There's nothing here, Peace, let's go," Jonah said when we all met up in the living room.

I was about to reluctantly agree when Tara, standing directly underneath the rafter from which the rope had hung, raised her full-moon eyes toward the ceiling.

"Guys…the rope…it's g-gone."

Chris reached out a comforting arm but thought better of it. Anyway, he was shaking too hard.

**

It was hours later, with all my farm chores done, when I returned…this time alone.

After the rope business, my fellow "ghostbusters" had vowed never to return to Bloodson Manor. But I couldn't get my mind off that pesky detail…or, more importantly, the elusive basement. I *had* to go back. Or go crazy speculating.

When I arrived, Bloodson Manor was colored in the reds and oranges of twilight. My steps around the house's perimeter were slow and deliberate as my eyes roved the foundation. I had gone over every square inch of the first floor looking and pressing and shoving and moving things in search of the hidden staircase that led to the basement, with no luck. I couldn't imagine that Reginald would have had the foresight or means to build something hidden behind a bookshelf like something in a Nancy Drew mystery. That meant the access had to be outside, but damned if I could find it.

I was on my second go-round, picking flowers as I went, when I stopped at the basement window. Something looked different about it.

The window was open.

Holy crap. Someone else was here. Or at least had been here and knew how to get inside.

I couldn't believe the window offered the only access to the basement, but it was the only choice I had if I wanted inside. The question was if I'd be able to get out once I got in.

A tight fear held me back. What if whoever had opened the window was still in there? I leaned my head inside the gap, listening. All was quiet. And dark. So so dark.

I slipped into the hole feet first, holding on to the

rotting window frame. The floor seemed forever away as I dangled, toes reaching for footing. A shower of mealy sawdust fell on my head. I knew I couldn't hold on much longer, lest the frame crumble, so I let myself drop. I crashed into a stool that tipped over on impact, then landed on my knees on a hard-packed dirt floor.

What the heck was a stool doing under the window? Unless...no, I would think about that later.

When I stood up, I knew what I had stumbled upon. I remembered learning in history class about root cellars in Colonial America. These spaces were used as storage for canning and preserving food in order to get early settlers through the winter.

A large table sat in the middle of the cellar cluttered with various rusted gardening tools. Cracked pots were scattered everywhere, along the walls and filling every empty inch of table. Woven baskets of what I assumed were petrified vegetables were lined up neatly.

I picked up a canning jar full of seeds that had a sliver of old fabric tied around the neck, with a word neatly inked across the twill:

Angel's Trumpet

Another jar, similar to the first, had another word handwritten across it:

White Snake Root

166

A third jar, the same as the others, had yet another word:

Hybrid Belladonna

This must have been where Cordelia worked her horticulture magic. I had read various entries where she described her experiments in cross-breeding plant species. She was an unheralded innovator, a brilliant woman crossbreeding plants in an era when women were expected to keep a tidy house and dote on her husband's interests, rather than cultivating her own. I knew nothing about botany, but my guess was Cordelia's discoveries predated those by her male counterparts decades later—yet they got all the credit. Some things never changed.

Down here, pressed into the belly of the earth itself, was a master gardener's dream. Cordelia's dream. Long, thin, rough-hewn tables, laden with oil lamps, lined another wall. I walked alongside it, reading the various plant names scribbled on paper scraps attached to jars. I imagined Cordelia cultivating her plants down here, nurturing them to life while experimenting on grafting projects.

A scuttle of tiny feet sent me back a few steps. It sounded like mice. As I ventured further into the root cellar, I heard scraping, like rats within the walls. Anything but rats, please! Except the walls were made out of brick, so the scraping had to be coming from somewhere else.

The ceiling lowered to the height of a crawl space as I followed the wall, probably due to the property's sloping terrain. Ahead of me was a wooden door—some kind of storage room, I speculated. Behind it the scratching grew louder.

"Hello?" I called out, my voice squeaking.

The scratching crescendoed into moans.

Although my eyes had adjusted to the growing darkness, the light from the sole window wasn't strong enough to carry this far into the underground cavity. And I had forgotten my flashlight, darn it.

Behind the door the sound intensified, like the wail of a wild animal caught in a trap. Every part of me wanted to run, until I remembered the bloodstain on the floor above us. It could be a person in danger. Someone who was hurt.

"Is someone in there?"

It was so deathly quiet that my ears were making up sounds that weren't there.

Until the groans turned and twisted into a word. A word I couldn't quite make out until it spoke again:

"Peeeeeace…"

Chapter 21

"Peeeeeace..."

Had I heard right?

Was it my *name* being spoken behind the door, or was I just hearing the tail end of some wraith moaning *rest in peace*...and it was about to float through the door and suck the life out of me?

Either way, I wasn't about to stick around and find out.

I just wanted to get the heck out of there.

Nighttime had fallen, swathing everything in an inky, impenetrable black. The scratching against the door grew more frantic behind me as I groped my way through the dark toward the window.

I could almost feel the fresh air beyond the window as I broke into a run. But I had forgotten about the table in the middle of the room as I slammed into it with my hip bone.

"Sonofabitch!" I screamed.

A moment later I heard the door creak open behind me. I jerked my head around, but I couldn't make out anything other than a moving shadow.

It was fight or flight. Flight won.

I felt around for the stool, grabbed it, and dragged it

over to the window. Thank God, it was just tall enough, with me on my tiptoes, to grip the edge of the window frame. Grunting, I pulled myself up, my feet scrabbling up the brick foundation. Halfway there! I was blinking the dust and wood flinders out of my eyes when I felt a hand grab one ankle and pull.

As my butt hit the hard earthen floor, my eyes couldn't register who—or what—I was looking at.

Chapter 22

"Get off of me!" I screamed, kicking and flailing on the ground.

One hard kick propelled my attacker across the room with a meaty whoomph. I sprang to my feet and scrambled across the floor toward the window. There was no time to right the overturned stool. This time sheer force of will got me halfway up the wall, until I glanced back briefly to lay eyes on the vague bundle hunched in the corner.

It was definitely human. Not a wraith.

I paused only long enough to hear a sob. A tiny question flickered through my brain. Maybe the person hadn't been attacking me after all. Maybe they were trying to stop me so I could help them. I relaxed my arms, allowing myself to drop back to the floor.

"Hey, are you okay?" I kept my distance in case it was a trap.

"Peace, I need help," the voice returned with a moan. "I think I'm dying."

Oh my gosh. I knew that voice. "Leo?"

I rushed to his side and gingerly lifted him to his feet. As I did so I felt the shape of a lighter in his pocket and tugged it out. I found the spark wheel and rolled it until it lit a flame. Glory hallelujah, I could see again! I held it up to Leo, being careful to avoid burning him. He kept scratching at his bare legs.

"Are you injured?" I asked, trying to get a look at his legs, but his hands kept frantically rubbing at the skin.

"No. I don't know. I don't think so," he said with quick breaths, then fell back to the floor and curled up.

"What happened?"

He shook his head violently. "I don't know. Just suddenly I felt…this weird sensation like bugs were crawling all over me and I was losing my mind. Shadows were, like, reaching for me. Then this feverish feeling just hit me out of nowhere. I don't know what's wrong with me!"

It sounded like the same symptoms of every other person who had died in this house:

Hallucinations.

Paranoia.

Then death.

I held his hands, stopping him from clawing his skin off. "Hey, there's no bugs on you, see? And no shadows. But I need you to try to stay calm and breathe. It's just you and me, okay?"

He looked up at me, imitating me as I drew long, slow breaths. For several minutes we sat on the ground breathing together, in and out. In and out. When he seemed as close to normal as he was going to get, I spoke softly.

"What were you doing here?"

He crab-walked away from me, back toward the door. "I can't tell you. You'll never speak to me again."

"Leo—"

"You won't understand..." He stood up, wobbly but at least upright.

I was tired of secrets and lies and coverups. I just wanted the truth. I stepped toward him, and he shuffled over to block the door.

"Are you hiding something in there?"

If he was, I couldn't imagine what it could be. This was Leo we were talking about. The same thoughtful boy who gave me Reece's Pieces, and the shy guy who was supposed to take me to dinner...tonight. Which we were both currently late for.

"Please don't ask me questions, Peace. I can't lie to you."

I exhaled long and slow, releasing my frustration. "How did you even get in here? Is the only way in through the window?"

"Well, there *was* a trap door through the pantry floor, but someone boarded it up. And the window was painted shut, so I couldn't get in that way. So I had to drop in using the old laundry chute."

He pointed to where a huge wooden box hung from the ceiling with an opening in the bottom. I walked over to it and looked up at it, seeing nothing but an endless black tunnel.

"How did you even fit in there?"

"It's a tight squeeze, even for a string bean like me."

"Then how do you get out? Certainly you don't climb your way back up."

He chuckled, such a soothing sound of normalcy. "I managed to pry the window open with one of the gardening tools."

Of course. That's why there was a stool under the window. And I hadn't considered the access being a door in the floor when I had searched for the stairs. In the failing light I noticed the decrepit ladder in the corner missing a few rungs.

Then it dawned on me. He was talking like he did this all the time.

"Wait—you've come down here before now? Do you come here a lot?"

"Not until recently," he answered cryptically.

"Were you down here the night Tara, Jonah, Chris, and I were here?"

He didn't say anything. So he was. That must have been what the thumping sound was—Leo climbing down the laundry chute.

"Just tell me why, Leo. I'm done playing games. I want the truth. I deserve that much."

In the flicker of the tiny flame I couldn't see my own feet, much less Leo's expression. But I felt it. A mistrust between us.

"I've been coming here because…"

"It can't be that bad, Leo. Just tell me."

Oh, how I would eat those words.

"I've been keeping a hostage alive down here."

Chapter 23

"What!" I screamed. My thoughts were swirling and whirling every which way. "Hostage? Are you on dope? If you're kidding me right now, I'll—"

"No, I'm for real! Somebody abducted this girl and chained her up down here. I was coming here to make sure she ate and to keep her alive. But today…" Leo broke down and sobbed. "I swear I tried to save her, but I couldn't…"

"Is she…" The question got stuck in my throat.

He stopped crying just long enough to say, "Dead? Yeah." Then he gasped and fell to the floor.

I was too shocked to go to him. A girl. Abducted a week ago. Then Emory McAlister's smile, those braces and choppy hair, flashed through my mind. The girl who stood up against corruption. Who spoke her mind…and my guess was that it killed her.

I thought of the bloody puddle in the dining room. Of the noises the first night we came to Bloodson Manor. Was that Emory's blood? And Emory's cry for help?

"Do you know who the girl is?" I asked.

He nodded. "I recognized her from school. Emily

something-or-other."

"Emory McAlister?" I clarified.

"Yeah, that's her."

"Do you know why she was abducted?"

"She had no idea who did it or why."

Maybe Emory had no idea who did it, but I did. I was more convinced than ever that Judge Valance was behind her abduction. He had the biggest ax to grind over her blog posts and her other attacks on his character, or lack thereof.

All I could feel was fury. I wanted Judge Valance to suffer for his misdeeds. It was too bad those old-fashioned public shamings I'd studied in school had gone out of favor. I'd love to see him shackled up in a pillory. Or tarred and feathered. Stoned to death by the innocent folks he'd sent to the pokey—I'd pay to see that!

"You have to turn your dad in, Leo."

"Whoa, aren't you jumping to a huge conclusion? What makes you think he's behind this?"

"Get real, Leo. Emory has been a thorn in his side for years. She's just about the only person who's been brave enough to speak out against his...questionable brand of justice."

Leo shook his head. "You're wrong. My dad had nothing to do with this."

"How can you be so sure? Because he's your father? Fathers aren't saints, you know. Not mine. And especially not yours—no offense."

"None taken. But you don't know the whole story yet."

"Then spill it!"

"Okay. I got a threat that if I told anyone about her, my whole family would be murdered. It can't be my dad. He wouldn't threaten his own family!"

"You don't think your dad is manipulative enough to pretend he's going to kill your family if you tell? C'mon, Leo. You know what your dad is capable of."

"Abduction and murder? My dad can't be that evil. Because if I'm the son of a murderer, Peace…" Leo was barely holding it together as he cried.

"How did you find her in the first place?"

Between sniffles and shaky breaths, Leo had calmed enough to speak, though his voice was husky and thick.

"It was by accident. A week ago I had come here to be alone after a big fight with my dad. I knew it was pretty much the only place in town where no one else would find me. When I heard screaming and thumping, that's when I found the trap door in the pantry, and followed the sound of her voice. I tried to break her out, but the chains were too thick and rusted to cut through. When I asked her who did this to her, all she knew was that she got an email demanding that she sabotage my dad's reelection campaign. She thought it was a joke because it's such a ridiculous demand."

I knew that while Emory probably hated Judge Valance's guts, and for good reason, she had way too many scruples to undermine his campaign. But I bet she was tempted.

"She didn't recognize the email address?" I asked.

"I guess not. Since she didn't know who it was, she ignored it. Plus, after the last time she outed my dad, MIT threatened to withdraw her admission and scholarship. She didn't want to risk losing that."

Leo paused and ran his hand over his face.

"Next thing she knows she's walking home one night and a van pulls up beside her, some masked guy gets out and grabs her, and he must have knocked her out with chloroform or something because she wakes up chained to the wall. She never saw a face or heard a voice or anything."

"How long was she here before you found her?" I couldn't imagine surviving a night in this cellar, let alone a week.

"I found her a couple days after she went missing. She had hadn't any food or water all that time. Her abductor just left her here to die, I guess."

Leo gestured to the door hidden in shadow, where Emory's body was chained.

"She was dehydrated, she looked terrible, and she was scared out of her wits. So was I! That same night I found her, I went home to get bolt cutters and planned to go straight to the police, but there was a note on my front door saying if I told *anyone* about the girl, my family would be tortured to death. Including the one person I cared about most. That's *you*, Peace! I couldn't let something happen to you. I...care about you. What would you do?"

His heartfelt words touched me. But to be honest, if my father was Judge Valance, I'd tell the cops for the mere purpose of getting him off this planet and into hell where he belonged. But that was just me.

"You're sure she's...not alive?" I didn't want to check her body myself, but I couldn't leave it up to chance.

"Yeah, I'm certain. Her body was stiff and cold when I got here. No pulse. I don't know what to do, Peace. I've been trying to hold it together for days, pretend nothing is wrong, but I can't keep doing it anymore. I can't leave her here. I can't tell the police. I'm terrified of getting my family killed. Or *you* killed. What do I do?"

I could hear in his voice that this was destroying him, and he was helpless to stop it. I went to him, reaching for him in the pool of black, and wrapped my arms around him. His cheek was hot and slick. His body trembled.

A body hanging from the rafter last year. A girl chained in a root cellar this year. A killer on the loose. Someone was targeting people and bringing them here, to this hell house, to die. As I held Leo's head, trying to soothe the tears, footsteps above us rattled the floorboards.

"Someone's here!" Leo whispered in a panic. "What if it's the person who's after my family?"

"How would they even get down here? The trap door is boarded shut."

"I don't know, but do you really want to find out?"

I absolutely did not, but I didn't know what to do. If we stayed, we could be trapped. If we ran, we could get caught...and trapped again. We sat in motionless silence while the footsteps, heavy like boots, walked back and forth, until they stopped right above us. Debris fell from the ceiling on top of us. I stifled a cough.

Then the footsteps resumed, heading across the floor above until they faded.

Chapter 24

Leo and I walked in expectant silence through the woods, listening for any sign of being followed. A crack of a twig. A rustle of leaves. Only when we arrived at the field behind my house did I finally breathe easy-ish again.

I couldn't talk about Emory's dead body chained to a cellar wall. I couldn't discuss what to do with her remains. It was too much for me. At least right now. So I asked Leo the question burning in my throat since I first realized it was him in the basement.

"Were you…high earlier?" I asked.

Leo looked at me like I was crazy, but it was a perfectly logical conclusion. From what I saw, and what I learned from all of the D.A.R.E. presentations our high school made us suffer through, he was exhibiting all the signs of being high on drugs. Especially psychotropics or hallucinogens like LSD. The Drug Abuse Resistance Education classes were supposed to scare teens away from drugs, but instead it seemed to build more curiosity around them.

Leo stopped dead in his tracks. "Are you asking me if I'm on drugs?"

"Well, you kind of looked strung out, Leo."

"You know my dad would literally kill me if I even *thought* something illegal, let alone *did* something illegal. Heck, he'd probably turn me into target practice if he found out I smoked cigarettes."

"I'm not judging one way or another. I just wanted to know," I said with a shrug.

"I would never mess with drugs, Peace. I'm sure you and everybody else in Bloodson Bay knows about my uncle overdosing a few years ago and almost dying. My dad never forgave him for that. It really hurt his campaign having a"—Leo paused, carefully choosing his words—"druggie deadbeat for a brother. Uncle Marv was pretty much kicked out of the family after he went to jail for dealing."

"I'm so sorry your family went through that. But I think you're being harsh on your uncle."

"Harsh? He almost ruined my dad's career! And the last time I went to visit him, I tried to tell him about my life, see if we could find some common ground, but all he could talk about was how our family let him down. What about *him* letting *us* down?"

I folded my arms and turned away. Leo's apple hadn't fallen far from his father's tree. "So you're saying your dad's career is more important than your uncle's life."

"No, I—"

"Not everyone who uses drugs is a deadbeat. They're people with feelings like everyone else. Sometimes they just have too many feelings and drugs seem like the only way to shut them off."

"I guess…but it's a pretty selfish choice, don't you think?"

"Yeah, I'm not saying it's a good choice, but it's also selfish to send your own brother to jail instead of rehab, and all for political gain. Look, all I'm saying is I don't judge another person's struggles." I ended it there before it turned into a fight.

Leo touched my shoulder gently. "You're right. And that means a lot coming from you. I guess you're one of the only people who understands since your uncle went through the same thing."

I felt like I was missing something.

"Are you talking about my Uncle Bernie? He never did drugs."

"Really? Last year, he almost died because he was high as a kite—and not on Pabst Blue Ribbon like usual. Something else. Something stronger. Don't you remember that?"

I shook my head. There was no way that could have happened without me knowing. Our family knew everything about each other. Except for my secret crush on Leo. And Chris's visit to the Slaughter Shed last year. And whatever Uncle Bernie was keeping from me. Okay, so maybe we didn't know *everything* about each other…

"Uncle Bernie may drink, but he doesn't do drugs."

"He tried to kill himself because he was hallucinating,

184

Peace. I assumed it was because of drug use."

Kill himself? Hallucinating? "Bull. I'm not buying it, Leo. You must be thinking of someone else."

"I *know* it was your uncle because I'm the one who cut him down from a rope when he tried to hang himself from the rafter in the Slaughter Shed. Your brother even saw him, but he took off instead of helping him."

That was the body Chris had seen—Uncle Bernie?

Leo rambled on, as if I wasn't flipping out right in front of him.

"I couldn't believe he was still alive when I found him. He had passed out so he looked dead at first, but luckily after I cut him down and performed CPR he came to. Thank God they made up learn it in phys ed, huh?"

"What makes you think he was on drugs, though?"

"He kept babbling that something was following him. He was clearly out of his mind, paranoid that someone was out to get him. He kept crying and saying how depressed he was. There was definitely some kind of drug use, because he was all sweaty and feverish."

Uncle Bernie, depressed? And using drugs? I knew that some people hid depression behind a mask of humor, and sure, he liked to drink, but how had he hidden this whole other side of him from our family? And why? I couldn't make sense of it.

Leo must have finally seen the alarm on my face. "Look, there's a lot of darkness that surrounds our families. It's no surprise if they're struggling. Some of us

185

are just better at hiding it than others."

"Why do you say that—that there's *darkness* surrounding us? What does that even mean?"

Leo got quiet for a long moment, then spoke in a hushed tone.

"There's something about our past that you don't know. A history that involves our families—mainly *your* family—that I'm not supposed to tell. My dad has spent his entire career hiding it, and I can't betray that trust."

"You're talking about the stupid curse and the stupid family feud that started with Reginald Bloodson and Edgar Valance, aren't you? I already know the story, Leo."

"It's more than just a story. I have proof."

"What kind of proof?"

"I can't tell you or else my dad would lose the only things he loves—his power. And if he loses that because of me...I hate to admit it, but he'd rather lose his son than his power."

"Then let's take him down! Your dad is corrupt, Leo. He needs to pay for his crimes!"

"No, Peace! He's my father. I can't do that to him. You don't understand because you have a nice, normal family. My family has more skeletons in it than a graveyard, but it's all I got. I hope you can understand that."

"No, Leo, I can't. One moment you're telling me you care about me, and the next you're telling me you have dirt on your crime family but won't use it. If you gave a crap about me, you'd do the right thing."

"What exactly is the right thing when it involves your family, Peace? You make it sound so simple. You must have a nice view from up there on your high horse."

"A girl's dead body is chained up inside a cellar, and it could be because of your dad. My guess is, he got wind that somebody was going to try to sabotage his campaign, and because of his past run-ins with Emory, he assumed it was her and had his thugs snatch her. Just think on that for a minute."

I felt hot tears well up, and Leo cupped my cheek with his hand. The moon had finally decided to show up, casting a bright glow that lit the entire field up.

"I...I care so much about you. That's why I can't just turn my dad in. I don't want anything to happen to you. My dad is the kind of man who would take everything I love away just to prove a point."

Love? Was Leo saying what I thought he was saying?

I couldn't explain what was coming over me that broke me into tears. Maybe it was the emotional overload. Maybe it was the feud between our families. Maybe it was the reality that we could never be together. Or maybe it was just exhaustion.

As all my anguish surfaced in my eyes, Leo leaned forward, gently touching his lips to mine. I allowed the softness, the warmth, to envelop me for a moment, until it all came crashing down as I realized I could never be with him. Too much hung between us.

I pulled away abruptly, pressing my palm to his chest.

"I can't."

"Why not?" he pleaded.

I didn't need to answer. We both knew it'd be too complicated in light of how much our families hated each other. Then I remembered the porch banister at Bloodson Manor:

L <3 P

"It was you, wasn't it? You carved our initials into the banister."

He nodded. "I've loved you as long as I've known you, Peace. And that will never change."

Leo's words sounded a lot like what Edgar had written to Cordelia before she died.

"We'll see about that," I said, wondering if it was true what they say, that loves conquers all.

Chapter 25

Chris and Jonah were in the basement playing *Goldeneye* on the Nintendo 64, while Tara occupied herself with a game of solitaire on the floor. My brain wouldn't shut off long enough to get through a single page of the book I had picked up from the library.

All I could think about were the secrets everyone I cared about had hidden from me. Along with a dead girl chained in the root cellar.

For a whole year Chris had kept tight-lipped about his terrifying experience, hiding it with video games and junk food. Uncle Bernie had tried to kill himself, masking his desperation behind jokes and drinking. Leo's own life had been threatened while he secretly tended to a killer's victim. When had our relationships become so dysfunctional?

The questions kept pouring out of me. What could cause my brother to keep something so traumatizing to himself? What could cause Uncle Bernie to feel so desperate that he'd want to leave this earth, leave *us,* behind? Who was hiding something so heinous that he'd kill an innocent teenage girl to stop her from uncovering it? *That* was the biggest question of all.

I was lying on the sofa watching James Bond infiltrate The Facility while Chris's fingers were punching the controller buttons and Jonah was screaming for him to watch out. For the last half hour they'd been absently plunging orange fingers into the bag of Doritos sitting between them, never taking their eyes from the screen.

"Hey, can you pass the chips before they're all gone?" I asked, even though I wasn't hungry.

Chris turned around and looked at me, licked his fingers, then reached in the bag and grabbed one.

Gross.

"Never mind," I said, rolling my eyes.

I glanced up from the paragraph I had read four times now when a pair of legs in beige Dockers blocked my view.

"Whatcha doin', kiddo?" my dad asked as he pulled up my legs, sat down beside me, and dropped my feet on his lap.

"Reading." I lifted up the book and showed him the cover.

"I was hoping to chat with you. You've seemed...off lately. Everything okay?"

Dad usually didn't come downstairs to the basement, which had been designated "the game room" when my parents relocated our shabby faded sofa and old tube television down here. So for him to seek me out, I must have been giving off some pretty worrisome vibes.

"I'm okay...I guess."

I added the *I guess* because I wanted to ask him the question that had been tormenting me all day: if he knew his brother had tried to hang himself last year. I didn't know how to tactfully bring it up, but teenagers my age were nothing if not tactless, so I just blurted it out.

"Did Uncle Bernie try to kill himself last year, Dad?"

He gawped at me, as if I'd just said Ronald Reagan was a closet Democrat.

"Whoa, Peace. You're going to need to explain."

I didn't want to be the one to tell him Uncle Bernie's personal business. I knew in my gut it should have come from his brother himself. But I planted the seed regardless. Someone should know. Someone other than me and Leo. Preferably someone who could get Uncle Bernie help.

"Never mind. It's just a rumor floating around, that's all. But you might want to check on Uncle Bernie, in case it's true."

"Ah, I get it. Since I'm mayor, people love to spread rumors like that. It's awful, I know, but they'll take advantage of any opportunity to sling mud and make our family look bad."

I hated how everything boiled down to politics with my dad. What about *people*?

"You think they'd start a *suicide* rumor? That's pretty dark, Dad."

"Politics can get dirty, honey. Especially when officials are up for reelection and in the middle of campaigning. If the opposing candidates can't get their way fair and square, some of them will stoop pretty low to stack the deck in their favor."

I wondered if Leo had made that story up just to get back at my family. I knew Judge Valance hated my dad, and the feeling was mutual. On several occasions my dad had publicly called him out on questionable rulings. It was no shocker that Leo could have been perpetuating some dirt his father had told him. But if all of it was a lie, then who had Chris seen hanging from the rafter?

There was only one truth, and only one person who knew it. I'd have to go to the source.

Chapter 26

When I arrived at Uncle Bernie's trailer, he was sitting on his stoop under a yellow porch light, moths fluttering around it, with a Budweiser in hand and four empties crushed at his feet. He looked up at me, cheeks flushed.

"If it isn't my little snoop of a niece," he said, without cracking a smile. "You here to rummage around my house and break stuff and then later lie about it?"

So he had found the crack in the ceramic box. I should have known he'd see it eventually.

"I'm sorry for lying about it. And for breaking Grandma's antique box."

"Are you sorry for taking that chest after I hid it *and* told you to stay out of that house?"

Jeez, nothing got past him!

"*You* hid the chest in the crypt?"

He chuckled. "I still can't believe y'all found it. You really are one hardheaded kid."

"But why did you hide it? What's the big deal with us checking it out? It's just an old trunk full of junk."

"You'll never learn, will you? You've heard the stories about the Slaughter Shed. You know about the town curse.

You've even seen what that house has done to people. The deeper you dig, kid, the bloodier your hands are going to get."

I shook my head. "You say all of this, but you never explain it."

"That's for your own protection, kid."

"What are you protecting me from?"

Uncle Bernie patted the other foldup camping chair beside him. "Cop a squat." After crushing his can against his forehead, he grabbed another one and popped it open. "There's a lot of family history you don't know about, and if some of it came out, it could ruin lives, Peace. I really wish you would let sleeping dogs lie."

"It's been forever ago, whatever you're referring to."

"It's not about me. It's about…stuff bigger than us. If some of the history came out, Peace…let's just say there are some big shots in this town who would kill to keep it hidden. Their lives depend on it. A young girl about your age is missing because she got too close to the truth."

Hold your damn horses. That girl couldn't be…

"Are you talking about Emory McAlister?"

Uncle Bernie's eyes lit up. "You know Emory?"

"I went to school with her. How do *you* know her?"

"I never told you this about me, but I know a thing or two about computers." I played ignorant and let him continue. "Emory and I ran in some of the same tech circles. Us computer geeks are a pretty small, tightknit community."

I felt the despair bubbling up. The first hot tear rolled down my cheek.

"Hey, what's the matter, kid? Do you know where she is?"

I had to tell him. If there was one person who could help, it was him. "Oh, Uncle Bernie..." The tears were pouring now. "She's...dead."

"No! That can't be. How do you know what happened to Emory?"

"Because..." I gulped back tears. "...because her body is chained in the basement at Bloodson Manor."

He flew up out of his seat and grabbed his chair and tossed it off the porch. Fragments of a shattered plastic leg bounced across the grass into the darkness. Then one by one he picked up the beer cans and threw them across the yard, screaming.

"I told her to keep her nose clean until college! I warned her the threats were real! Why wouldn't she listen? Oh, Peace, this is never going to end..."

"What's not going to end, Uncle Bernie? Who did this to her?"

"That's the problem, Peace. I don't know who. At first I thought it was Judge Valance, because everyone knew she dug up dirt on him in the past, but now I'm not so sure."

"I don't understand. Why don't you think it's him?"

He hesitated. He had some bombshell to drop, I just knew it.

"Uncle Bernie, I need to know. A girl is dead because of this."

He stared off into black nothing, then fixed his gaze on me. "It all started when I hacked into Judge Valance's email last year just for practice…and because he's a douchebag who deserves it, y'know? Anyway, I found some incriminating emails involving blackmail and him paying some cops off, as well as some shady real estate transactions. There was a lot."

Uncle Bernie stopped, as if he was considering telling me more, then he shook his head. "Anyway, I mentioned it to my hackers group—there's a few of us here in town— and Emory just wouldn't let it go. It was like she had a personal crusade against Judge Valance. But after he found out and threatened to get her full ride to MIT withdrawn, she promised me she'd stay out of trouble this past year. She promised…"

Uncle Bernie was pacing at this point, wearing a path across the porch.

"Eventually I ended up telling Judge Valance what I knew, and that I had proof. He said he wanted to meet me on June 27 of last year. Guess where?"

"Bloodson Manor," I hazarded a pretty educated guess. The night Chris found him—only he didn't know it was him—dangling from a rafter.

"Yep. So I show up. We end up meeting outside in the garden. I tell him I'll *lose* my evidence if he resigns his judgeship. He assures me he'll right his wrongs and clean

196

up the system if I keep my mouth shut. And if he can't follow through, then he'll step down. We shake on it and over the past year he's kept his part of the bargain. So when I heard that Emory went missing a week ago, it didn't make sense..."

It was hard to imagine Judge Valance cleaning up his act, but I guess miracles could happen.

"Did Judge Valance have anything to do with what happened to you last year? In the living room at Bloodson Manor?"

He turned his face toward me so quickly it was scary. I instantly regretted asking.

"What do you know?" he demanded.

I was suddenly too afraid to speak.

"Someone told me that you, um, tried to..." I couldn't push the words out. It felt too private a question.

He nodded, as if he'd read my mind.

"Hang myself?" he finally spat out.

"So it's true?"

His eyes glazed over, staring into the gloom with a faraway look. Then he snapped back to the porch and looked me square in the eyes.

"I'm guessing your *friend* is Leo Valance. And yep, I admit I did. Wasn't successful, obviously."

"What happened?" I asked.

"Well, I had been drinking something fierce before my meeting with the judge because I was nervous. Sometimes a beer...or twelve...calms my nerves. After he left, I passed out in the garden. When I woke up I was feeling crazy. Paranoid and seeing things. Thought a ghost was after me. It was nuts. And then I was thinking about the judge hurting my family, and this wave of depression hit me hard. I just wanted to end it all. So I cut off a piece of rope from the tree swing in the front yard and went inside and convinced myself it was the only way to stop the demons. I had never felt anything like that before, and I hope to God I never feel it again."

I jumped up from my chair and rushed him, hugging him harder than I'd ever hugged him. I squeezed his big belly, sobbing into his shirt. I never wanted anyone to feel that kind of hopelessness. That kind of desperation.

"Hey, kiddo, it's okay. I'm still among the living. Don't you go crying over me."

"But you could have..." I wiped my nose on my sleeve, rejecting the thought.

"But I didn't. Thanks to your friend Leo, of all people, giving me CPR or I'd be playing a harp right now. Who would have thought a Valance would rescue a Bloodson?"

"I don't understand why you did it though. Are you depressed?"

"No, kiddo. I mean, we all go through crap days, feeling sorry for ourselves and all that. But this was something else. Something I can't explain. I was seeing shadows moving. Reaching for me. My body was cold and hot all at the same time. You know, our ancestors had a long history of mental illness. Going as far back as

Reginald Bloodson, the stories have included hallucinations, and then when he killed his whole family, and his youngest son took his own life...we can only assume there was something broken inside because it's just not normal to want to kill your whole family."

"Well, sometimes it's normal," I tried to joke. "Especially when your brother eats all the Doritos and doesn't save you any."

Uncle Bernie laughed lightly as a sprinkle dotted his bare arm from the edge of the porch awning, then another and another. "Looks like rain."

I didn't move. Even as raindrops pelted my shoulders, I couldn't let him go, not yet. So I stood there hugging the rustic Santa, and wishing he were the real Santa and could make all my troubles go away.

We stepped back under the metal roof, listening to the tap of raindrops overhead. My voice sounded raw when I spoke again. "Is that why you drink so much now?" I hoped I wasn't crossing a line, but I felt like we had reached a new level of honesty.

"Hm." He didn't say more than that for a long time. "Maybe. I guess I do it to forget what I had done. I never gave it much thought. But when I really think about it, I started drinking a lot more after your dad and mom asked me to look into renovating Bloodson Manor—as if I ain't got enough on my plate."

"What? When did this happen?"

"Oh, a few months ago. They said to keep it on the QT

for now. They've been wanting to add the house to the historical sites registry, but it needed some work done to meet the standards. We had been kicking the idea around of turning it into a local tourist attraction."

"Isn't that kind of morbid?"

"Sure, but people love a good tragedy, and a house of horrors could bring in money for the town. We need it bad, with that real estate snake Corbin Roth buying up all the properties around here and pushing tax-paying locals out of town."

Everyone in Bloodson Bay knew the name Corbin Roth, and everyone hated him. Except for Judge Valance, who benefitted from Roth's real estate schemes that drove away families and crippled our town's economy.

"Look, honey, I'd appreciate if you kept this between you and me. I don't want anyone knowing. If your dad was to find out…it'd break him."

Oh crap. I had already hinted as much to Dad.

"Are you ashamed of it? Because you shouldn't be."

Uncle Bernie scratched his chin. "It's complicated, honey. What I did isn't something to be ashamed of, but it's hard on the people around you. I guess what I'm trying to say is shit's a reality of life, and you just need to make sure you take care of yourself and get help if you need it. There's nothing wrong with asking for help."

"Then why are you hiding what you did instead of asking for help?"

I got him there, and he knew it.

The moonlit mist turned to white streaks as the sky opened up and Uncle Bernie ushered me inside. He fetched a towel for my hair as I stood shivering in the living room.

"You gotta wait out this rain before you head home. In the meantime, wanna see something cool?"

"Sure." I had no idea what Uncle Bernie deemed cool, but I could suffer a few minutes while he showed me.

He led me to his computer room, which I pretended I had never seen before.

"Wow, what's all this?" I faked.

"This, my dear girl, is where my hacking magic happens."

This actually was surprisingly cool.

"Can you show me how you hack into something?"

His face scrunched up and I could see a no forming on his mouth...

"Pleeeeease? I promise it'll stay just between us."

The downturned lips meant yes in Uncle Bernie speak as he pulled out two rolling chairs and we sat. His fingers flew across a keyboard, popping a billion letters a second across the screen.

"Okay," Uncle Bernie said, lacing his fingers of his outstretched hands and cracking his knuckles, "we're going to hack into the county jail."

As he demonstrated each step, he tried to explain back doors and servers and a whole bunch of techy mumbo-jumbo. I followed enough of it to get a loose grip on what he was talking about, but the best part was seeing the list of inmate names beside their convictions and sentencing. A familiar name briefly caught my eye, disappearing as Uncle Bernie scrolled down the list.

"And that is your crash course on how to hack a local government database." And this was only the beginning of what my uncle could do. He plugged a tiny rectangular device into the computer tower. "This is called a pen drive. I saved this whole process on here so all I have to do next time is plug this in and it'll automatically hack into the county jail system. Nifty, huh?"

"Can I have it?" I held my palm out, grinning slyly.

"What for?"

"I dunno. Just because."

"Do you even have a computer?"

"Uhhh...nope." I pocketed my hand.

"If anything ever happens to me"—his voice dropped to an undertone—"someone listed on this pen drive is probably responsible." Then he chuckled as I smiled uncomfortably.

"I'm so impressed, Uncle Bernie. Why are you working as a farmhand when you should be running a dot-com company?"

"Farm work gives me a sense of accomplishment. I'm saving horses, giving them a second chance. This computer stuff I just do for fun."

I sat back, staring at the black screen covered with tiny green numbers and letters as the rain slowed outside. Where it had before been practically power-washing the window, now it was just a light spray.

"You should probably get home before your mom reports you missing," he joked.

Which of course made me think of Emory, a girl who was never coming home because she was chained to a wall in a root cellar.

"What is it about Bloodson Manor that drives people mad and causes so much death?" I mumbled, staring out the window toward the woods.

Uncle Bernie pulled out the pen drive, powered off the computer monitor, and stood up, heading out the door.

"Whatever it is, kid, stay away from that place. Something ain't right about it. In the meantime, somebody has got to let the police know that poor Emory is lying dead in Bloodson Manor." He stroked his grizzled beard, sighing. "And I guess that somebody will have to be me. It'll be quite a blow to her family...I know they've been hoping against hope she'd be found alive and well."

Selfish as it sounds, I didn't want to be incriminated for concealing a crime, or whatever the charge might be. I didn't want Leo implicated either. "What are you going to do, Uncle Bernie?"

"I guess I'll give the police an anonymous tip. That'll have to do for now. But the whole sordid story may have to come out...someday." He heaved another heavy sigh. "Now get on home. I've got some thinkin' to do. Maybe some prayin' too."

As I walked home through the drizzle in contemplative

silence, I knew in my deepest being that something about the house was hurting people. But I'd have to go back to the very beginning to figure out what it was.

The Diary of Cordelia Bloodson

June 27, 1837

My dearest Cordelia:

Today I mark with inexpressible sadness the anniversary of your passing, exactly one year ago.

My deepest apologies, dearest, for having read your diary, to say nothing of the sacrilege of adding to it my own inadequate words. But I miss you terribly, and so I find the sight of your crisp, flowing hand, your eloquent words, a salve to my aching soul. Perhaps it was divine intervention that I even found this book in the secret compartment in the linen chute. Your ingenuity and craftmanship have always amazed me! It was by mere happenstance that door popped open as I bumped that massive old steamer trunk you refused to part with on the corner of the wall. That is when I spotted the gap against the chute with this book tucked inside. What a gift to read your thoughts after all this time.

205

I miss you terribly, as do the children, but I refuse to let my loneliness swallow me whole. I vowed to you before you passed into glory, to live among the angels, that I would forever honor you with my life, that I would raise our boys to be compassionate, good-hearted, and reverent. And I have so far been true to my word.

Much has happened since you left us. My dear sister Gertrude postponed her plans to move to Savannah with Edgar in order to care for the children. She showers Sigmund with her particular favor, doting on the lad night and day. She has been a great help, as has Edgar, who seems eager to ensure I recover in full from the anguish of last year. His tinctures and medicinals offer some relief, though at times they befuddle my mind.

Like today.

My brain feels heavy, filled with fog, as all I have wanted to do is sleep. Gertrude assures me it is the weight of the anniversary of your death upon me. My mind craves slumber, for only in the arms of Morpheus can sorrow be forgotten — for a little while.

This evening, in memory of you, I will take the boys to the cliff's edge, gaze upon sun sinking into the ocean, as we did the day I proposed to you, and tell them the story of how we pledged for one another our undying love. I shall do this every year in remembrance of you, my darling, so that none shall forget the moment you claimed me as yours, and I claimed you as mine.

Always yours, until we are reunited in heaven, my love.

Reginald

Chapter 27

Always yours, until we are reunited in heaven, my love, Reginald had written. If only he had known it would be later that night.

The word *wow* formed on Tara's lips as she closed Cordelia's diary. Tara was speechless, which was unheard of…and maybe even a first.

After a long night reading Cordelia's account of the history that plagued my family, and that haunted Bloodson Manor, I came to the conclusion that I couldn't follow Uncle Bernie's advice. I couldn't stay away. I couldn't stop digging. It wasn't how I was wired.

When I had called Tara at home this morning, she retracted her boycott against all things Bloodson Manor and agreed to help me. Then she showed up at my doorstep before I'd even had a chance to finish eating my Lucky Charms. I'd never get too old for that marshmallowy goodness.

After Tara helped herself to a bowl of the "magically delicious" cereal, properly eating all the marshmallow bits and leaving the toasted oat puffs floating in lukewarm milk, we headed to my room to do some digging. It took us all the way to this very last diary entry—not from Cordelia herself, but an elegy from Reginald, written one year after his beloved wife's death—to come to the conclusion that something terrible had happened, but it wasn't what everyone had assumed all these years.

"Are you thinking what I'm thinking?" she finally asked, handing me the book.

"That this is all the proof we need to show that Reginald didn't kill his family?"

"Damn skippy," Tara agreed. "He sounded mentally stable on the day that he died, right? And determined to take care of his children. So what happened between the time he wrote this letter and later that night when he and his kids died?"

We might never know. It was a gaping hole in the timeline that we couldn't fill with anything other than speculation.

"And if Reginald didn't kill his family," I added, "who did? And how—without getting caught?"

"You're thinking it was murder, not an accident." Tara was reading my mind now. "But wouldn't investigators back then have questioned it?"

I set the diary down, considering Tara's question. I imagined nineteenth-century detective work was pretty primitive compared to what you'd see on a *Law & Order* episode. And sadly, there were no preternaturally perceptive fictional sleuths like Sherlock Holmes around.

"All they knew was a recently widowed husband and

four children were found dead at the bottom of a cliff. If there was no witness to a crime, they probably let it go. The Lizzie Borden case is a prime example of this, unsolved to this very day. Talk about missed opportunities. The police found a pail of bloody rags in the basement and took ol' Liz at her word when she said she'd been menstruating—a squeamish subject the cops didn't want to pursue. On top of that, she didn't give consistent testimony in court, and yet she still got off!"

"Who's to say they all didn't slip and fall?" Tara speculated. "We don't even know who found their bodies. If we knew that part, we might be able to put all the pieces together."

The problem was, so Mom told me, that Bloodson Bay was such a backwater town that no major newspapers deemed the deaths, suspicious or not, worthy of coverage. With no one pursuing answers, the mystery went unsolved, so the gossipmongers slapped a murder-suicide label on it and called it a night.

No matter what the legend said about our family, there were too many inconsistencies. And too much at stake.

"I still think it was Dr. Valance who did it. We know he and Cordelia had history together. He even admitted they were in love and she broke his heart. I imagine since it was a small town and the options were probably slim, Gertrude was probably not even his second choice, but more like his last resort. But I can't figure out *how* he managed to kill Reginald and all of the kids. You'd think a couple of them would have managed to run away."

I picked up the diary, re-reading a passage Reginald had written that had hung around in my brain:

"His tinctures and medicinals offer some relief, though at times they befuddle my mind...My brain feels heavy, filled with fog, as all I have wanted to do is sleep."

"Wait a minute," said Tara, musing aloud. "He said he was sleepy...which is a side effect of certain drugs. And it can hit you pretty quickly if your body isn't used to it. So if Dr. Valance drugged Reginald, he might have drugged the kids as well. And since Reginald already planned to watch the sunset with his kids at the cliff, maybe all Dr. Valance had to do was...give a little push."

"It makes sense. He was a doctor with access to any kind of drug he needed. So he offed Cordelia first, figuring that if he couldn't have her, no one could. Then a year later he took out Reginald by medicating him and the children until they were too out of it to realize they were being shoved over a cliff during their memorial to Cordelia. Of course Edgar couldn't leave any child witnesses, and since Sigmund was just a year old, there was no reason to kill him. Which made him the lone survivor. I think we figured it out!"

Tara continued threading the logic to today. "And if the Valance family knows this and it became public knowledge, Judge Valance's career would be over. It's the perfect smear campaign…"

"And the perfect reason he wants to keep it hidden!"

It made sense that it was the big secret Leo was referring to that could ruin the Valance family's name. A stain like that was hard to remove, especially for a controversial public figure like Judge Valance.

We had everything we needed to clear my family's name—and destroy our enemy's reputation while we were at it. Reginald's parting words showing a mentally stable man on the day he died. And Edgar's brokenhearted love letter to Cordelia, giving motive for murder. We could easily dethrone Judge Valance with this, and restore the Bloodson family's good name.

As I was about to close the book, a particular phrase struck me as significant:

"Here Reginald refers to the steamer trunk that Cordelia *refused to part with*. Why do you think she was so attached to it?"

Tara glanced over at the chest sitting in the corner of my room. "She had mentioned before that she'd hidden Reginald's shaving kit in it for protection because she was scared. But she never specifically said she was scared of Reginald. What if she wasn't scared of him, but rather of Dr. Valance?"

Tara had a good memory…and an even better point.

"Why would Cordelia be scared of Dr. Valance? She never mentioned anything concerning him in her diary."

"Unless she did but we didn't catch it," Tara said.

212

I had remembered reading little details here and there that seemed out of place. What if they were clues she had left behind for whoever read her diary after she was gone? I thumbed back to a key passage to refresh my memory.

"In her very first entry for June, she mentions a sense of foreboding, that something bad is going to happen. Then she talks about seeing things at night, like someone was in her room. She's got this sense of dread that keeps growing throughout the entries. Maybe you're right, and that dread was over Dr. Valance. He was her doctor, after all, so he was always around."

Tara gasped. "And maybe she knew he had spiked the medicine bottles with poison, which is why they were hidden in a secret compartment. That's got to mean something that Cordelia went to great lengths to hide them."

Tara had noticed a crusty residue in one of the anti-hysteria bottles. That might have been the remnants of dried poison. I opened the chest; the two bottles were resting on top. I removed the unmarked bottle and removed the lid. Sure enough, the inside was coated with something flakey.

"Look at this. You're right—this was how he managed to poison them," I speculated aloud. "Using the anti-hysteria medicine. I wouldn't be surprised if this unmarked bottle was used for Reginald, since men could be diagnosed with hysteria too. Cordelia even wrote about her concern of hysteria being contagious."

Had we actually figured it out?

I needed to know for sure, and I had a gut feeling I would find it in the attic at Bloodson Manor.

Chapter 28

As we wandered through Cordelia's garden heading toward Bloodson Manor, I promised Tara we would be home before dark. I didn't want to be here either, but I was confident my answers were here. The truth was here. Everything was here.

Holding the diary close to my chest, I noticed an unusual specimen, unlike any flower I'd ever seen, with trumpet-shaped blooms. I bent down and plucked one and inhaled its sweet scent. How odd that something so beautiful and fragrant could surround a house with a history so dark and troubled.

Tucking the blossom behind my ear, we headed inside. This time the dried pool of blood held a whole new significance—Emory's death. The chest held a whole new terrible truth—Dr. Valance's evil. The house held a whole new terrifying darkness—a friend turned villain.

We climbed the stairs to the second story, then headed through the doorway that led up to the attic. The daylight brightening the rest of the house grew dimmer with each step upward, until we reached the very top, where just enough light poured through the tiny window to illuminate what I had come here for.

The framed artwork. The face of Dr. Valance, seen by Gertrude for who he really was. I had not recognized the chiseled chin and perfect nose, so distinctive in the sketch Gertrude had done, before now, as they were hidden behind a terrible scowl and demon-black eyes staring back at me. I wondered if Gertrude had been expressing through her artwork her true vision of the man who tortured her. Was this how she saw her husband—as a grotesque monster? His face was a study in pure ugliness, incongruously wreathed in beautiful flowers. Beautiful flowers that looked extremely familiar…

"Isn't that the same flower that's in your hair?" Tara asked.

I plucked the blossom from behind my ear and held it up to the picture.

It matched! Same flower, same glossy, toothed leaves.

Like poison ivy leaves. Or the castor oil plant. Both of which my mother warned us kids to watch out for when we went galivanting through the woods due to their poisonous nature.

"Crap!" I exclaimed. The cutting dropped from my fingertips to the floor. I understood so much now.

"Tara, I think I know how Dr. Valance was poisoning them!"

Tucking my fingers up my sleeve, I carefully picked up the plant, making sure I didn't touch it with my bare skin—although it was too late for that! I darted across the room, Tara chasing me with a bewildered expression while I searched every table, trying to remember where I had found it—the sketchbook.

I finally located it sitting on a table, just as I had last seen it. I flipped it open to a series of pictures Gertrude had drawn of Cordelia's plant hybridization projects. Gertrude had helped catalogue all the botanical experiments in this book. Tara's cocked eyebrow told me she had no idea what was running through my mind, so I explained.

"Cordelia was a botanist, and she told Gertrude how she had been experimenting with various plants to create hybrids, some of the first of their kind. You can see some of them in these pictures."

I pointed out a sketch depicting the exact flower that I held, with a handwritten caption above it: *Belladonna cross-pollinated with Angel's Trumpet*

"The result is this plant." I lifted it for Tara to see. "We need to find out what angel's trumpet and belladonna are. I have a feeling this will help us figure out what kind of side effects contact or ingestion would cause."

Within an hour we were sitting in my bedroom, sketchbook open to a detailed illustration of several plants Cordelia had cultivated, pulling out various *Encyclopedia Britannica* volumes for each name. I found the first one and read the entry aloud:

Angel's Trumpet, also known as Devil's Snare, is one of the deadliest hallucinogenic plant species that can

217

cause a wide range of symptoms, including fever, itching, paranoia…visions…and death.

It was everything Cordelia had described happening to her, to Reginald, even to Gertrude. The entries for several of the other plants listed, including White Snake Root and Wolfsbane, were equally toxic. What the heck kind of experiments was Cordelia doing? It was no wonder everyone was seeing things!

"All of these can cause depression and intense panic…even hysteria."

"In some extreme cases they can cause death," Tara said, eyes widening in horror.

Another picture showed a deadly nightshade hybrid, which had been commonly used to induce sleep before anesthesia was discovered. That must have been how Edgar got everyone sleepy enough to shove off the cliff without triggering any alarm.

The final piece of the puzzle clicked into place. Leo's erratic behavior in the root cellar…Uncle Bernie's sudden depressive state after passing out in the garden. The yard was blooming with these toxic hybrids, and certainly both had passed through them into the house. I had to tell them they weren't going crazy—it was simply a side effect of the plant. Which meant that the Slaughter Shed wasn't haunted.

The town wasn't cursed. It was simply an experiment gone deadly wrong when it landed in a vengeful man's hands.

Chapter 29

I raced over to Uncle Bernie's trailer with Tara straining to keep up. "Where are we going?" she called out behind me.

I didn't waste time telling her. I didn't stop to explain. I had one priority, and that was setting everything right for Uncle Bernie.

I darted up the porch steps, too eager to bother knocking, and burst through the door. He'd forgive me for rushing in when he heard the truth.

"Uncle Bernie! I have something to tell you!" I yelled, standing in his tiny entryway.

When he didn't answer, I heard the television in the living room and headed past the kitchen to the living room, where I found him lying on the couch watching NASCAR.

"Uncle Bernie?" I whispered.

Last year Uncle Bernie had taken his first plane ride ever, flying to Arizona to watch his beloved Pittsburg Steelers "open up a can of whoop-ass" on the Dallas Cowboys in Super Bowl XXX. The Steelers lost. Now he seemed asleep, covered in the black-and-gold Steelers blanket—he called it his "crying towel"—he'd brought home as a souvenir. It was pulled up over his face. Only his closed eyes were exposed.

But this was news worth waking up for. I stood beside him, shaking his shoulders.

"Uncle Bernie, wake up!" I cooed. "You're going to want to hear this."

But he didn't move. Didn't respond. I pulled the blanket down and sucked back a scream. He was as pale as an eggshell. His lips were frozen in a macabre stillness. Runnels of blood snaked through his matted beard.

"Uncle Bernie!" I yelled, shaking him violently. When I pressed my ear to his chest, I didn't hear him breathing, didn't hear anything other than my own panic drowning everything else out. I turned to Tara, pointed at the phone hanging on the kitchen wall, and screamed, "Call 9-1-1! He's not breathing!"

"The ambulance is on the way," Tara told me a minute or two later, though I had lost all track of time. "And I called your parents. They're coming over now."

The more I looked at him, the more dead he looked. His fist hung limply off the couch cushion, clutching something. I gently pried his fingers open and pulled out a pen drive. The one he had saved his county jail hacking program on. I held it in my palm, still warm as if it held the last of Uncle Bernie's body heat. This was a message from Uncle Bernie to me.

If anything ever happens to me, someone listed on this pen drive is probably responsible, he had warned me.

Uncle Bernie wanted me to find this, and I knew what he would want me to do with it.

I hadn't heard the rush of bodies storm in through the front door, shoving me aside as an EMT took over while Mom guided me into the kitchen so I couldn't watch. I didn't *want* to watch them try to resuscitate my uncle, or hear them announce my uncle's time of death.

Instead, I slipped into the computer room alone and fell to my knees. Everything was falling apart and I didn't know how to pick up the pieces. I wanted to cry my freaking eyes out. But all I could do was silently rage.

Crumbled on the floor, the walls began to spin. The floor began to tilt. My head swam, my body ached, my mind raced. And soon the shadows came alive, creeping toward me, reaching out, trying to suffocate me.

Somewhere in the recesses of my brain I knew the poison of the flower I had touched was wreaking havoc on my system, but I couldn't call out. My voice had stopped working. My throat had closed shut. And everything inside me screamed silently for help to an empty room.

I was stuck somewhere between high and terrified, unable to establish footing on either plane.

Eventually the visions dulled and the panic abated and the rage subsided to tears. When I had exhausted every tear—it could have been seconds or minutes or hours later, they all felt the same to me—I rose to my feet, sat down in Uncle Bernie's rolling chair, and dropped my head into my hands, two balloon-like appendages that looked larger than life.

I bumped the mouse with my elbow and the computer screen zipped to life. I plugged in the pen drive. Although the screen looked distorted, I could see the jail hack program running. Through my brain's numbness I barely grasped the list of recently released convicts—with a familiar name at the very top.

I didn't get the chance to process this earthshaking news for more than a moment before the computer room door swung open and my mom rushed in.

"Peace, you need to go home right now and stay put. Your uncle's been stabbed."

Chapter 30

If whoever stabbed Uncle Bernie didn't kill me first, my mother would do the job. Because I shouldn't have snuck out of the house with a killer on the loose. And I shouldn't have gone alone without protection. And I *definitely* shouldn't have shown up on the doorstep of the person who might be connected to the attack.

But somehow I knew I was the only one who could stop this. The only one determined enough to expose the secrets and put an end to the madness.

Leo's bedroom window was on the second story of their brick mansion, the glass lit up in a golden yellow. Like a lovesick teen in a John Hughes flick, I grabbed a piece of gravel from the driveway and threw it at the glass. Grabbing someone's attention this way was a lot harder in real life than it looked in the movies.

The first shot hit the wall right below the window.

The second shot was too light, not even making it to the house.

The third shot had perfect aim, but as it cracked against the glass, I could already see where a small chunk had broken out of the pane. *Oops.*

At least it got Leo's attention, though. A moment later his face appeared behind the glass, and I waved my arms, hoping to entice him to come outside without me having to scream his name. Recognition dawned on his face, and he held up a finger, signaling me to wait.

Cars passed by on the street, and I could hear the faint sounds of voices talking inside the house a mere ten feet from where I stood hiding in the bushes. I prayed no one would see me, especially Judge Valance, who I was certain would slap me with a trespassing charge simply to punish me for being a Bloodson.

The swish of the massive front door opening scared me up against the brick where I hid behind a holly bush, the barbs pricking my skin.

"Peace?"

Thank God it was Leo.

"I'm over here," I whispered back.

Leo rounded the corner and found me in the shadows, then he pulled me by the hand toward the backyard where we would stay out of view of the street.

"What's going on?" he asked when we finally settled into a dark corner of the yard.

"I can't talk long, but my uncle was stabbed tonight. Do you know anything about it?"

His face dropped into a genuine frown. "Oh, Peace, I'm so sorry. But no, I know nothing about it. My dad and brother have been home all night. It wasn't them, if that's what you're thinking."

I didn't know what I was thinking anymore. It could have been the plant toxins or shock of finding my uncle near death, but my brain was everywhere and nowhere at once.

"Look, Leo, I know all about the bad blood between our families and the history there. I know your ancestor Dr. Valance was in love with Reginald Bloodson's wife. And I know he poisoned and killed the Bloodsons. So I know…enough. And I also know why your dad would kill to keep it quiet, since he'd do anything to hang onto his power and influence."

"Peace, I begged you to stop! Why wouldn't you listen to me? You're going to get yourself hurt! Haven't enough people suffered over this?"

"Are you blaming me for my uncle getting stabbed? Because you can't ask me not to want the truth. It's the reason our families have been hating each other for 160 years. Don't you think it's time to put the war to rest?"

Leo sighed in defeat. He knew me well. And he knew I was right.

"Come with me," he urged. "You know part of it, but not all of it. There's a big piece you're missing."

"Where are we going?"

"You'll see."

I didn't know if I could trust him. My uncle was fighting for his life right now over this very secret. But I couldn't resist the pull of the truth, the need to uncover it all and lay it all bare. I needed to stop it, even if I had to

226

pay the price. Because Leo was right—too many had already suffered over this. It was time to free the ghosts.

I followed Leo through his backyard toward the woods where a dirt path led deep into the heart of the forest. Further and further we walked in silence, away from anyone who could see or hear us. Away from town. Away from witnesses. In terrible isolated silence.

My legs were starting to ache when we finally came to an area I recognized. I knew these woods. They backed up to the rear part of our property. Leo led me to the small wrought iron gate.

"What are we doing at my family's private graveyard?" I asked as I followed Leo through the gate.

"We weren't always enemies, Peace." He gestured to the three Valance graves surrounded by Bloodsons. "At one point we were family. I want to find that with you. Whatever it takes."

"How, Leo? I don't even know if I can trust you."

"Okay, fine. I'll tell you the truth. Even if it makes you hate me, at least you'll know I would never again lie to you. Vic did let your horses out to distract you so you'd go home—but he never expected them to run all the way to the cliff. And we did follow you to Bloodson Manor that night, mainly to make sure you didn't find *this*."

He reached into his pants pocket and pulled something out.

"This belongs to you."

He handed me a locket, and I recognized it

immediately. It was the one I had seen in the attic in the musical jewelry box that first night. Then I remembered that night at Blockbuster, and the telltale bulge in his pants I'd gone gaga over. He'd had it all this time. But why?

"I saw this locket in the attic. What are you doing with it?"

"There's a letter inside that tells a story. Only it's not just a story. It's all true. It's what you wanted to know about the truth behind the Valance-Bloodson Feud."

"How did you find this?"

"I had discovered it a long time ago when I just a little kid messing around in Bloodson Manor. I remember showing my dad, and he told me to destroy the letter. I realized it must have been pretty important, so I returned it to the attic for safekeeping because I didn't want him to find it."

I opened the large locket and found the folded letter written on cotton rag paper, expensive and exquisite to the touch, and beautifully preserved.

"What exactly is this?"

"This is me choosing you, Peace. Over my family, over my dad. It's all the proof you need to destroy my father for what he's done."

I opened the letter and read with hungry eyes.

From the Pen of Doctor Edgar Valance

July 3, 1837

To my wife Gertrude,

After much contemplation, I have chosen not to write adoring platitudes to you as I often have over the past year. Rather I pen this letter as a plea. A plea to release us both of the guilt of this secret, lest it destroy everything that remains of us. Have you felt the burdensome weight of this sin as I have? Over the past week it has become so leaden that it stakes my soul to the ground. Thus I beg of you to hear me out.

Let me return home and confess. Let me throw myself to the wolves in penitence as I expose what's been done. We once vowed to carry this secret to the grave, but let me propose a new tack. One forged of complete honesty, no matter the sacrifice. Is not integrity more valuable than gold?

To prove my devotion to you after all the pain I have

caused you, I bring you good news. During my time here in Savannah, I have studied new fertility treatments that have proven wildly successful. Let me give you the sibling you desire for Sigmund. In exchange for this I ask only one thing:

Let me confess to the murders once and for all.

If your answer is no, I resolve to hold this secret within my breast until my dying breath out of devotion to you, for I put us in this wretched place. I owe you this much after my myriad sins. But I leave you with one final consideration:

Consider your son Sigmund. One day he will discover what has been done to his father, to his brothers. Future generations of Bloodsons will seek vengeance against Valances, kin against kin until our family is torn asunder. And the feud will rage on like a festering wound that my confessional could stanch once and for all.

I believe there is only one rocky path forward, and I am willing to take it. Will you free me to do so?

Earnestly Yours,

Edgar

Chapter 31

Leo was right—this letter could expose everything as it revealed what had started the battle between the Bloodsons and the Valances. It could set history right. And it could knock Judge Valance off his ill-gotten throne.

But it wasn't enough.

It couldn't bring Uncle Bernie home from the emergency room. It couldn't prove who stabbed him. And it couldn't raise Emory from the dead.

Who cared who killed who 160 years ago? All that mattered right now was finding out who killed a teenage girl and stabbed an innocent man.

"I can't believe our families felt this was such a big deal that they've all been waging war against each other for a century and a half, and hiding this for all these years. Is this really worth all of that hate?"

"Peace, I don't want this"—Leo waved to the letter clutched in my hand—"to come between us. You know I like you, a lot, and I don't want our family's stupid drama to be our drama. We can break the cycle."

"Except that my uncle could end up dead because of the family drama, Leo."

Then suddenly something Leo told me came to mind.

"When you were threatened to keep quiet about Emory, the note said he would go after *the one person you cared about most*, right?"

Leo nodded. "Yeah, that's right."

"Then my uncle gets stabbed—which is pretty darn close to *me*. How did the attacker know the person you cared about most was me?"

Leo was quiet for a long moment. "I honestly don't know."

"Who did you tell about your feelings for me? Does Vic or your dad know?"

He shook his head. "No way."

"Who else would know?"

Emory's killer and my uncle's attacker *had* to be connected. There was no way around it. It was also most likely the same person who locked us in the crypt. So if I put all the facts together, the person was someone Leo confided in about his feelings for me, who owned a V for Valance belt buckle, and most likely had a criminal record if he could leave a girl to die and stab a man without remorse.

A criminal.

I reached into my pocket and pulled out Uncle Bernie's pen drive, his last message to me. I mentally conjured the top name on the recently released convict list:

Marvin Valance, Released June 10, 1997

Just a few days before Emory went missing.

"Did you ever tell your Uncle Marv about me?" I asked breathlessly.

"Yeah, why?"

"Because it fits, Leo. He knew you cared about me. He's a Valance—he has that same belt buckle, right?"

"Yeah, bu—"

"Let me finish! He wanted your dad's life ruined just like your dad ruined his. That's why he threatened Emory—hoping she could use her tech skills to sabotage your dad's reelection campaign. It was no secret she had dug up plenty of dirt on your dad and had been an outspoken critic of his tactics. So he figured she would jump at the chance to take him down. Marv was wrong. Emory was much too ethical to stoop to sabotage. So when she refused to cooperate, he just left her in the cellar to die. And targeting me by locking me in the crypt was his warning to you to keep your mouth shut. Don't you see? It was Marvin Valance all along."

"Holy sh—"

"We have to go to the police now, Leo, before someone else gets hurt!"

"Are you absolutely sure it's him?"

Absolutely sure? How could I be? I didn't have DNA testing or concrete evidence. All I had was my intuition.

"You know what—never mind, Peace. I love you. I trust you. And I'll do anything to prove it to you."

Yeah, I'd heard Leo heard say those three Gigantic Little Words that every girl longs to hear. I wanted to say, while batting my eyelashes, of course: *Uh, would you mind repeating that?* But all I could think of was Marv going after my brother or Tara…or Jonah.

"Then help me put your Uncle Marv behind bars."

Chapter 32

It was a miracle that Uncle Bernie made it through surgery alive. In a medically-induced coma, but at least alive. Although he was unable to tell the cops who attacked him, I knew. And Leo knew. And we told them everything, including the whereabouts of Emory McAlister's body, and all the details we knew about her abduction. A warrant was issued for Marvin Valance's arrest.

Apparently Uncle Bernie had never gotten the chance to phone in the anonymous tip. When the detective asked me why I hadn't reported that Emory's body could be found at Bloodson Manor, I had no good answer. I couldn't tell them that I'd been so caught up in solving a mystery—so wrapped up in *myself*—that I'd forgotten to be a decent human being. I hated myself for that. Guess I had some growing up to do. A lot, actually.

Finally I was back in my bed with nothing left to solve. So I thought. But the words from Edgar's letter to Gertrude swirled incoherently around in my head, taunting and torturing me. Something in his confession didn't add up. I sensed the answer was there, if I only read between the lines—and if I was smart enough to grasp the clues.

Clicking on my bedside lamp, I gave in to the urge and found his July 3 letter tucked into the locket that sat on my dresser. I noted the date. I reread his words. I considered the melancholy tone. Then I paused on one particular line:

I have chosen not to write...as I often have over the past year.

And then another:

Let me return home and confess.

Yes, there was something there I had missed. I pulled out Cordelia's diary. A common theme coursed through each entry leading up to her baby's birth—and her death.

A growing anxiety as her delivery date grew near. Followed by paranoia. Hallucinations. Similar to the symptoms Reginald experienced, as well as Uncle Bernie and Leo and myself, under the influence of the very plants Cordelia had created. And who was there to comfort her?

Gertrude.

At the root of every entry, in the background of every page, was Gertrude. Caretaker. Child-rearer. Midwife. They all trusted her. They all were close to her. And yet Gertrude had reason to hate them all. Her husband secretly loved Cordelia. The children were a constant reminder of her own fertility struggles. And her brother gave her over to a man who would endlessly torture her body.

The secrets crashed into me. The details collided. And the truth revealed itself.

Dr. Valance had killed no one. It couldn't have been him, for he was away in Savannah on an apprenticeship perfecting Gertrude's upcoming fertility treatments the entire year prior to Reginald's murder. Which left Gertrude home alone with Reginald and his sons. And available to murder them all.

She had first killed Cordelia with poisonous devil's snare-laced anti-hysteria medicine the day she gave birth. Then a year later, after Reginald and his sons were drugged into a sleepy suggestible state using deadly nightshade, she pushed them off the cliff while Dr. Valance was down in Georgia.

Gertrude Bloodson-Valance, the victim and the villain. Jealous over her brother's success. Resentful of her sister-in-law's children. Betrayed by her husband's love for another. Traumatized over her husband's medical abuse. It was enough to drive any woman mad. Certainly enough to push a woman to kill.

I followed Edgar's train of thought, seeing beneath the surface: his desire to confess to Gertrude's crimes out of guilt for what he had done to her. He had broken both her heart and her body; he owed her this confession at the very least.

But this led to the mystery of Sigmund's death thirty years later. Had Edgar accurately predicted what would happen? Had Sigmund discovered what Gertrude had done to his family, then fought with her—as witness testimony from his wife suggested? I imagined that fateful hysterical moment as Gertrude pushed him off the cliff after he threatened to expose her, the woman who had raised him alongside her own son, as a killer.

I could only guess exactly what had transpired, but it would have been enough to spark a feud when Gertrude took out Reginald's last remaining son.

All of this meant that the Valances no longer had anything to hide. It was a Bloodson, after all, who had started the curse.

I had two choices. I could clear the good name of Reginald Bloodson and the murderous acts he was charged with from beyond the grave. Likewise, the Valances' reputation could remain unblemished by any stigma. This could finally end a long-standing grudge that had been built on assumptions.

Or I could keep Gertrude's secret, let her brother carry her guilt, and let the curse of Bloodson Bay live on.

Chapter 33

I sat in a semicircle around the campfire with Tara, Chris, and Jonah, watching the flames lick the cool air, a contented silence enveloping us in its warmth. We were still on cloud nine after getting the news that Uncle Bernie had finally come out of the coma. He remembered nothing of the attack, and was blissfully ignorant of the past several days' events, but I would never forget.

Leo's squealing on his Uncle Marv had branded him a family outcast, but on the bright side, it solidified his romantic chances with me. His father, who had won his reelection bid handily, had forbidden Leo to see me. But since when did any teenager let their parents dictate who they could love? We were born rebels, and we would live and die as rebels.

The *Bulletin* ran a sensational front-page story on Emory McAlister's untimely death, hailing her as a fearless public crusader. Her funeral had drawn an overflow crowd. Call me a coward, call me a hypocrite, but I didn't attend. But a couple days later I did place fresh flowers on her grave at Bloodson Bay Cemetery. And I will again.

Jonah's hand reached across the space between our thighs, cupping my palm in his. I looked at him sadly. I hadn't told him about Leo yet...and I knew it would break his young heart.

"After everything we've gone through, is there any chance for us?" Jonah whispered, as the crickets nearly drowned out his voice.

I squeezed his hand, holding it on my lap.

"I need you as a friend right now, Jonah. Can't that be enough?"

I felt his hand twitch, as if he was about to release me, but his grip remained firm.

"Yeah, if that's what you want, it's always enough."

Hanging down against my heart was the locket, with Dr. Valance's letter tucked inside. A secret that I would keep for Gertrude. Woman to woman. Because when it came down to it, hadn't she suffered enough?

Across from me Tara rested her head on Chris's shoulder, and he stroked her hair tenderly. Tara fiddled with a Butterfinger wrapper, trying to peel it open. She held it up to Chris.

"Can you help me with this?" she asked.

"I'll always help open your candy wrappers," Chris teased, "as long as you give me a bite."

Tara chuckled. "I know. That's why I asked."

I smiled to myself. She knew what she was doing, and I had a feeling Chris did too. Showing him she needed him. And he ate it up like...well, candy.

"You know I love you, don't you?" Chris murmured against her hair.

"What?" Tara said, lifting her head to look him in the eye.

"Since the second grade. And I think I'll always love you, no matter what people say about me being too young to know what love is. And I think you might love me too."

She leaned forward and kissed him on the cheek.

"I don't think we're too young to know what love is."

Then she grabbed his face, closed her eyes, pulled him toward her, and kissed his lips. He sat in stunned silence, eyes the size of grapefruits, until she released him.

"You didn't punch me!" Chris's mouth dropped open in mock surprise.

Jonah and I glanced at each other and laughed.

"I love you too, Chris Christie," Tara cooed. "You and your silly name."

"Does that mean you'll be my girlfriend?" he asked.

"I suppose," she answered, resting her head back on his shoulder.

"You guys know that young romance rarely makes it past high school, right?" Jonah said.

"Put a sock in it," Chris bristled. Then, tenderly: "What now, Tara?"

She shrugged. "I guess you open my candy bars from now on...until we grow old and die."

"Together?"

"Of course! Together. Forever and always."

They were cute. Sweet. And so naïve it was sickening. But they'd grow out of it.

As for me, I no longer felt that my life was so rudderless. In the past couple weeks I'd experienced more drama and excitement than most people do in their entire lifetimes.

And I planned to write one helluva book to about it.

**

The mysteries are only just beginning!
Dive into more thrills and chills from the
IF ONLY SHE KNEW SERIES by visiting
www.pamelacrane.com.

About the Author

PAMELA CRANE is a *USA Today* bestselling author and wrangler of four kids who rescues horses and has a writing addiction. She lives on the edge and writes on the edge...where her sanity resides. Her thrillers unravel flawed women with a villainous side, which makes them interesting, and perfect for doing crazy things worth writing about. When she's not cleaning horse stalls or cleaning up after her kids, she's plotting her next murder.

Join her newsletter to get a free book and updates about her new releases and deals at www.pamelacrane.com.

Enjoy what you read?

Then You'll Love *Little Does She Know*

WOULD YOU DESTROY YOUR BEST FRIEND TO SAVE YOUR HUSBAND...IF HE'S DONE THE UNSPEAKABLE?

Ginger Mallowan embodies everything the 1980s stand for, from big hair to power suits to "Material Girl"...until her son disappears during a beach walk one night. That's the moment girls don't want to have fun anymore, and the moment she starts hunting for answers.

Now Ginger's hair is a bit flatter, her power suits packed into the attic, and her dance steps to Madonna lack the energy of better days. She hasn't found—or forgotten—her missing son, and she's only survived the grief thanks to her neighbor and keeper of secrets, Tara Christie.

Except for Ginger's darkest secret of all...about what happened the night her son disappeared. But that vow of friendship is tested when Tara is jarred awake one night by a scream coming from next-door, where she finds Ginger standing over a dead body. Even stranger, Tara's husband is nowhere to be found.

As the investigation shakes the town to its core, and Tara's husband is arrested for the murder, Tara must choose between proving her husband's innocence or protecting Ginger's past. *Little does she know* they're about to stumble down a twisty path that could destroy them all.

An Instant Bestselling Book Club Pick:
A Slow Ruin

April 1910. Women's rights activist Alvera Fields mysteriously vanishes from her home one night, leaving her newborn baby and husband behind, the case never solved.

April 2021. On the anniversary of her great-great-grandmother's disappearance, Alvera's namesake Vera Portman vanishes in an eerily similar manner.

Six months later, the police recover a girl's body. While the family waits in the horror of finding out if it's Vera, Felicity Portman clings to hope that her missing teenage daughter is still alive. Despite all odds, Felicity senses a link between the decades-apart cases—a mother feels such things in her bones. But all suspicion points to the last person who saw Vera alive: Felicity's sister-in-law, Marin.

Marin, with her troubled past.
Marin, the poor woman who married into the rich family.
Marin, the only one who knows Felicity's darkest secret.

As Felicity makes a shocking discovery in Vera's journal, she questions who her daughter really is. The deeper she digs, the more she's ensnared in the same mysteries that claimed their ancestor in a terribly slow ruin.

A Karin Slaughter Killer Reads Pick:
Little Deadly Secrets

The deadliest secrets lie closest to home...

From *USA Today* bestselling author Pamela Crane comes an addictively readable domestic suspense novel about friendship, motherhood ... and murder.

Three best friends. Two unforgiveable sins. One dead body.

Mackenzie, Robin, and Lily have been inseparable forever, sharing life's ups and downs and growing even closer as the years have gone by. They know everything about each other. Or so they believe.

Nothing could come between these three best friends . . .
Except for a betrayal.

Nothing could turn them against each other . . .
Except for a terrible past mistake.

Nothing could tear them apart . . .
*Except for **murder**.*

One of POPSUGAR's Must-Read Thrillers:
The Sister-in-Law

She stole my husband. So I'd steal her life.

The Wife

Lane won Candace's heart over chocolate martinis and karaoke. But weeks into their whirlwind marriage, Candace realized Lane came with burdensome baggage in the form of his possessive live-in sister and her eerily watchful six-year-old son. Lane had a secret that seemed to hold him hostage, and Candace would do anything to uncover it.

The Sister-in-Law

Harper was the kind of woman who cooked homemade meals and dusted under the furniture. It was the least she could do for her brother after her husband's mysterious death, and Lane took her and her kids in. Then Candace showed up like a tornado passing through, threatening and destructive. But Harper had other plans for her new "sister," plans Lane could never find out about.

The Husband

All Lane had ever wanted was a white-picket-fence life. The wife. The two-point-five kids. The happy little family. Everything seemed to be falling into place with Candace ... until Harper's jealous streak got in the way, again. But choosing between his sister and wife would be costly ... and knowing Harper, the price would be blood.

What would cause a woman to murder her own family? Find out in *Pretty Ugly Lies*

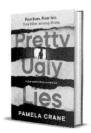

Jo's idyllic life would make most people jealous. Until the day her daughter is abducted, and the only way to find her is to unravel her dark past.

Ellie is a devoted wife . . . until she discovers the pain of betrayal. Now vengeance is all she can think about.

Party girl Shayla knows how to hide her demons. But when she's confronted with a life-shattering choice, it will cost her everything.

June knows suffering intimately, though the smile she wears keeps it hidden.

Soon the lives of these four women intersect—and one of them is about to snap . . .

Over 100,000 copies sold!
The Art of Fear

A fearless detective. A stolen child. A killer just getting started.

Ari Wilburn's life ended long ago—the day she watched her little sister die in a tragic accident and did nothing to stop it. Crippled with self-blame and resented by her parents, she stumbles through life … and onto an unexpected clue that casts doubt on whether the death was accidental.

Now a psychological wreck, Ari joins a suicide support group where she meets Tina, a sex-enslaved escapee whose daughter is missing and her long-lost father dead. Suicide, police ruled it. But Tina suspects foul play. As a bond develops between the women in their shared loss, they're dragged into playing a dangerous game with a killer.

A serial killer with a deadly message.

Faced with a murderous wake-up call and two possibly linked deaths, Ari's investigation puts her next on the killer's list. But she's never been one to back down from a fight.

Needing closure, Ari must face her demons and the killer behind them … or lose everything she loves.

A Twisty Romantic Thriller
The Admirer's Secret

From friends … to lovers … to murder.

Haley Montgomery is chasing a dream she can't quite catch, to become a successful screenwriter. She'd do anything to escape her family's failing vineyard and unrequited love for her best friend Marc. Then the opportunity of a lifetime comes to her small town as renowned film producer Allen Michaels offers her a ticket to a better future…but not without a cost.

It can't be coincidence that as Haley begins working with Allen she starts receiving strange threats. It can't be fate that Marc at last wants something more when she's already got one foot out the door. And it can't be safe when Haley uncovers a bone-chilling secret about why Allen showed up in her obscure town.

When a body is found buried in Marc's backyard, Haley doesn't know who to believe anymore. Allen claims Marc is dangerous. Marc claims he's been framed. All she knows is that no one can be trusted, especially not her own heart.

Haley thought she was chasing a dream, but now she's running from a nightmare.

Printed in Great Britain
by Amazon

33302767R00148